Shadow Of the Faolan

Book 3 of Ard Magister

I0679820

Laura J. Underwood

Shadow Of the Faolan
Laura J. Underwood

First Edition Copyright © February 1, 2024

Published by Yard Dog Press at Kindle

ISBN 978-1-945941-46-7
Shadow Of the Faolan
First Edition Copyright © Laura J. Underwood, 2024

Yard Dog Press
710 W. Redbud Lane
Alma, AR 72921-7247

http://www.yarddogpress.com

Edited by Selina Rosen
Copy & Technical Editor Lynn Rosen
Cover art by Steven Parks

First Print Edition February 1, 2024
Printed in the United States of America
0 9 8 7 6 5 4 3 2 1

The Chronology of the Tales of Ard-Taebh

Novels

Dragon's Tongue (Meisha Merlin, 2004)

Wandering Lark (Yard Dog Press, 2010)

The Black Hunter (electronic edition from Embiid, 2002; print edition included in *Chronicles of the Last War*-Yard Dog Press, 2004)

Willowherb (novella in *Chronicles of the Last War*-Yard Dog Press, 2004)

Ard Magister (Yard Dog Press, 2002)

Demon in the Bones (Yard Dog Press, 2016)

Shadow Of the Faolan (Yard Dog Press, 2024)

Short Fiction and Novellas

Bogie Woods And Other Tales of Conor Manahan (chapbook collection of short stories from Yard Dog Press, 2001) Now part of *Tales from Keltora* (Yard Dog Press, 2012)

Shadow Hart (novella in *Keltora, Land Of Myth*, an electronic collection of short fiction from Embiid Publishing, 2001)

Wyrd (novella in *Chronicles of the Last War*-Yard Dog Press, 2004)

Shadow Lord (chapbook novella-Yard Dog Press, 2003) Now part of *Tales from Keltora* (Yard Dog Press, 2012)

Gather My Bones (electronic novella-Jintsu E-Books, 2003)

The Dancing Stones of Nevermhor (novella in *Tangled Webs and Other Imaginary Weaving* from Dark Regions Press, 2002)

Dedication

For the Fans who have never given up on me.
Thank you for your loyalty.

Table of Contents

ONE

"Howt awa!" Conor shouted and jerked up his plaidie so abruptly, Eithne rolled off the pallet they shared. She landed on the straw-covered ground with a jarring thump and a squeak. Conor nearly trampled her in his rush to seize up his long dirk and reach Rhoyd's side.

Blessed Brother, not again! Eithne groggily stumbled to her feet. Conor stabbed his dagger in the ground and tried to pin thrashing limbs and quiet the lad's terrified howls. Rhoyd's cries carried as loudly as the low of a panicky cow and echoed off the braes.

We'll wake the whole world, she thought.

Already, lights filled the windows of the neighboring croft. The old farmer who owned this cow byre they sheltered in suddenly charged through his door clothed only in his hastily bound ells of a marriage-shortened plaidie. The frayed edges flapped like batwings as he ran across the ground towards the open side of the byre.

"Where's the beast?" he shouted.

She noted that he was armed with little more than a rake and a lantern, but he waved it about like a pole arm, flashing the light over the scene.

"What's wrong? Has a demon got the lad?" he asked.

Eithne sighed and rolled her eyes. "Superstitious old..." she muttered, then stopped herself before she launched into an old tirade about Keltorans and their bogies. Conor's efforts to awaken Rhoyd "gently" were proving fruitless. Whatever nightmare devoured Rhoyd's sleep would not let go of the lad. Grumbling, she snatched up the farmer's bucket by the door of the byre and dipped it into the cattle's water trough. Without warning, she turned and doused both husband and son in a bath of cold.

Conor cursed and lunged off to one side. Rhoyd stopped shouting and sat up, gasping for air and coughing.

"Howt awa, woman!" Conor glared at her. "Are ye trying to give me and the lad a chill?"

"Not to mention, dampening me good hay," the farmer said, though his eyes crinkled with merriment.

Ignoring both, Eithne dropped the bucket and knelt on the other side of Rhoyd. His wet black hair looked like rivulets of ink coursing over his face and back.

"Sorry, lamb," she said, "but sometimes extreme measures are called for."

Eithne took up the one dry end of Rhoyd's blanket and wiped his face. Conor muttered curses about insane women as he used the end of his plaidie to dry himself.

"Are ye all right, lad?" he asked as he reclaimed his dagger.

Rhoyd looked up, blue eyes large in the lantern light, and slowly nodded. "Sorry," he muttered. "It was that dream again."

Conor thinned his lips in a tight line. The muscle of his jaw twitched.

"Sorry, indeed," the farmer groused. "What about my hay?"

Conor turned to the man with a surly glare. "We'll give ye a silver sgillinn to pay for the hay," he said. "I'm certain there's still plenty for the kye."

The farmer put out his meaty hand. Conor stiffened, then muttered under his breath as he scrounged for his sporran and produced the coin. Clutching it, the farmer marched back towards his croft where his wife and children stood crowded into the doorway, all eyes agog.

"Auld thief," Conor muttered.

"You should have offered him brass," Eithne said. "He

can buy a hundred times this hay with that silver."

Conor pinched his face into a scowl at her then managed a kinder lock for Rhoyd. "Well, at least this dream canna be blamed on me," Conor said. "What's got ye all a blether these nights, lad. The same dream?"

Rhoyd shrugged in a noncommittal manner. "It's not just a dream," he said. "It's like...like when I see things that are going to happen."

"Well, you've naught to fear as long as I'm around," Conor said. "Though I'm not so good at stopping the woman here from trying to drown us both."

"Just you remember that," Eithne said and finished her chore, catching Rhoyd's chin. "None the worse for wear, I think. Only a little damp."

"A little," Rhoyd said, and his mouth bowed into an infectious smile and glanced at his wet bedding.

Eithne smiled and planted a kiss on his forehead. "Rogue," she muttered.

"Since his bedding is wet, he'll have to crawl in with us," Conor said. "May be a tight fit."

"There's plenty of room," Eithne said, "as long as we make you sleep in the wet hay."

"Yer heartless, woman. No respect for yer man."

"Do you think I want to curl up under your sodden plaidie now?" she said.

Conor laughed. "All right. Ye two can share the pallet and I'll take the hay. Just hope I don't catch me death."

Eithne nodded, rising to return to her bed, pulling Rhoyd along.

She could not help but notice the haunted look that hid behind the lad's eyes.

Was this an omen?

The rhythmic munch of hay close by woke Conor the next morning. He rolled over and nearly kissed the nose of the cow grazing close to his head. With a snarl, he jerked back. The bovine turned skittish and retreated from the byre, leaving a fresh cow pat in its wake. The odor hit Conor's nose.

"Horns!" he hissed as he rolled away from the stench. It was a wonder he had not pissed his plaidie in the process.

With a groan, Conor sat up and ran fingers through his hair to extract bits of hay. Bogies must have lodged themselves there, what with the tangles they left in his hair during the night. A man should know better than to sleep in a cow byre under the Ferlie Moon. Late summer was on them, and Conor had been watching the spiders weaving closer to the ground than usual. Autumn would soon be sending its chill across Keltora early this year, and Conor wanted to return to Wenthorn in Loughan before two more moons passed. Winter was coming early to be sure.

He grunted and glanced around. Where were the woman and the lad? The horses were still tethered outside. Hens strutted around the yard. The kye he'd startled slowly crept back to the byre again as though weighing its options.

Crawling to his feet, Conor continued to search. The pallets were gone. No doubt packed away for travel. All that remained in the byre were his things.

"Eithne?" Conor called. "Rhoyd?"

"They's with me woman in the croft."

The voice startled Conor. He reached for his long dirk and turned to seek the owner of the voice. The old farmer--Conor vaguely recalled that his name was Lorn--leaned through the small window in the back of the byre and grinned.

"Yer as jumpy as a fox in a kennel o' hounds, m'lord," Lorn said. "Of course, if I had a lad what screamed in his sleep every night, I suppose I'd be a bit jumpy meself."

"He doesn't do it every night," Conor said defensively. Though he reminded himself that the lad had been nocturnally vocal for nearly a moon. Always the same dream, the deformed beast like a wolf that tried to run the

4

lad down and kill him. At least, that much Rhoyd had told Conor.

Lorn merely shrugged. "He's fey, isn't he?"

"What?" Conor said. "How do ye mean that?"

"Yer lad, he's one of the mageborn," Lorn said and scratched under his stubbly chin.

Conor frowned. They had met many who distrusted magic and mageborn in their travels, but it was rare to find men of closed minds here in Keltora where the mage blood was even in the line of the kings.

"What of it?" Conor asked, and hoped his tone carried a strong enough threat.

Lorn merely shrugged again and went back to his raking. "No need to tie knots in yer plaidie, m'lord. I've a cousin with mage blood in him. He had bad dreams when he was about that one's age too. In fact, my aunt used to dose him with chamomile and sage in warm wine every night to keep him from waking the rest of the kin. May haps yer herb wife should be told this?"

Conor started to deny that Eithne was merely an herb wife. She was a True Healer, a servant of Diancecht, but here in the highlands, old ways and names were still held sacred. The farmer meant no disrespect for all his gruff ways.

Ye'd think I'd remember such things after all this time.

"What are my wife and lad doing in the croft?" Conor asked.

Lorn paused from raking. "Settling up with my missus, I imagine."

"Settling up?"

"More like bartering," Lorn said. "Yer herb wife has an elixir what lets colicky bairns sleep, and my missus is of a mind to make some for her youngest sister. The lass birthed a babe that gets it fair often. So, yer herb wife is teaching my missus the manner of the making."

Conor nodded and started collecting his things.

"So where be ye headed?" Lorn asked. "If ye no mind my asking?"

"Wenthorn, in Loughan," Conor said.

"Loughan?" Lorn said. "Long ways off for a Keltoran ta be heading this time of the year. You'll be wanting the south road, then."

Conor stopped and frowned at Lorn. "The south road? Through Tamhasg Wood? That's more than a wee bit out of the way. I want to be over the Highland Ranges and into west Loughan before the next moon. I was going to take the road past the Faolanwold."

Lorn tensed. "That would not be a wise road, m'lord," he said. "Not even for a muckle man like yerself."

"And why's that?" Conor asked.

"Been things happening on the moors around Faolanwold that would make even a strong man tremble."

"What manner of things?" Conor asked.

"Deaths," Lorn said. "Women and children and livestock eaten whole by a beast no one can stop."

Conor felt his eyebrow shift. As a lad, he had heard strange things about Faolanwold. About a cavern where a pack of wolf men lived. Of men who thought themselves to be kin to the beasts for which the Faolanwold once took its name. But these were only stories. He had passed through there many times and had nary a bit of trouble.

"What sort of beast?" he asked.

"Some say it's a wolf as large as a pony," Lorn said. "It wanders about the moors below Ben Faolan, scattering sheep and eating the shepherds. Sometimes it is said to steal into the village at night and take wee ones from their cribs."

"Someone should hunt it down and kill it," Conor said.

"Been tried, or so my cousin tells me. The hunters went missing, at least until someone found what was left of them and not missing."

"Is this the cousin with the mage blood?" Conor asked.

"Nay," Lorn said. "His younger brother. He's a travelling smith and trades regular in the villages about the edge of the moors surrounding Faolanwold, and he gets his news from the villagers there when he travels about to repair their cauldrons and knives. They say none of them will cross the moors now, no matter what goods they needs."

"When did all this start?" Conor asked.

"About a moon ago," Lorn said.

Conor frowned.

A moon ago was when Rhoyd started having that dream.

When they reached the crossroads at midday, Rhoyd could not help but notice how tired Conor looked. Dark circles had been growing deeper under Conor's rich green eyes. Even now, they had the hooded, dreary look of a man deprived of sleep.

My fault! Rhoyd thought. *No one was getting much sleep these days. And I am to blame.*

He sighed and turned his gaze upon the landscape that surrounded them. The rolling moors made it difficult to see too far, but this crossroads sat on a high enough patch of ground that it afforded them a glimpse of the heights of the misty mountains several leagues away. Beyond those mountains lay the tip end of Loughan's southwesterly border where it was wedged in between Keltora and Scarrif. Conor had shown Rhoyd this on the maps when they reached Caer Keltora with a caravan from Dun Ferlie in the far north.

Rhoyd had liked Dun Ferlie. Mountains, rocks--it looked just like most of Keltora, but there was magic in the place as well, and it sang to Rhoyd in a delightful manner. He liked getting to see all the places Conor had lived in his years training with the militia. Rhoyd had played tag and wrestled with Conor among ancient standing stones while Eithne watched and shook her head.

But as Conor said, they could not live on air, so he looked for work. They rode with a caravan to the High King's City, and while Eithne visited the Temple of

Diancecht to pay her respects to her god, Rhoyd and Conor had explored the city. It was so huge Rhoyd had wondered how anyone ever found their way. The great cities of the north were nothing by comparison.

Rhoyd sighed again as his thoughts darkened. That caravan had been the last full job Conor managed to find. From Caer Keltora, they had picked up another and stopped in Ben Brae, near Conor's birthplace.

That was where all their troubles began.

Rhoyd heard wolves howling on the moors one night, and then he had the dream. In it, he was being chased by a beast that look half wolf and half man. It came after Rhoyd, deformed jaws slathering, stinking of the rot of the grave. He ran from the monstrosity, stumbling over rough terrain where boulders jutted like broken teeth among the uneven clumps of heather and sedge. Behind him, a forest of bare trees, petrified by some horrid event of yore, stood as sentries inside the gates. A mountain keep lorded over the landscape, its broken door forming a cyclopean eye, black and baleful among the rocks of the ruins. Overhead, a moon as bright as winter snow cast pale milky light and turned the world bright blue. Here and there, swatches of blood stained the ground. As Rhoyd ran, he often stumbled over headless, half-eaten corpses.

He fled, uncertain what else to do until the creature bore him down on the heather, its snapping jaws lunging for Rhoyd's throat. He fought against it, snagged the grotesque jaws with his bare hands, trying to push the creature away.

It was then he glimpsed a figure standing off to one side. Dressed in armor under a long cloak, the creature had a human's body, but its head was that of a wolf or a fox. It stood and watched the struggle, tears flowing from lupine eyes.

And as it watched, it sighed and whispered, "You should never have challenged the dark, boy, for now the dark things will seek to escape and bring back the Mother of All Shadows and the Night of the World, all because of you."

Those words cut into Rhoyd like a dagger. The will to live suddenly left him. He ceased struggling against the fiend that pinned him to the heather and calmly met his attacker's feral gaze. The beast reared back, uncertain, hesitant for only a moment.

Then its jaws closed.

And that had been when Rhoyd screamed last night at the croft.

Before? He could still remember the angry shouts of the men the first time he awakened them with his screams. Looks of distrust followed Rhoyd around the next day. They muttered curses at his back, unaware that he could hear every unkind word.

The second night, Rhoyd's cries were even louder. And on the next day, the caravan master had thrust four silver sgillinns into Conor's hands and asked them to leave.

Conor had not looked pleased, for his wage was supposed to be five silvers a day. But Eithne seemed convinced they would find another caravan to work. They stayed south of Ben Brae in an old inn that served a decent fare. Conor mellowed after downing an ale. He told funny stories that made Rhoyd laugh and forget the terrors that frightened him in his sleep.

All seemed right in the world until Rhoyd had the dream again. He woke everyone under the roof--some swore he woke others for half a league around the inn as well. Come morning, the innkeeper told them not to come back to his house should they pass that way again.

Rhoyd tried not to cause any more trouble, but every night, the dreams invaded his sleep. They grew stronger to the point that Eithne suggested a sleeping draught might be in order.

That helped for nearly a sen'night. Conor found work again, and they followed yet another caravan that traveled down the road. Under Eithne's herbal draught, Rhoyd slept too deep to dream. But in the morning, he could barely crawl out of his pallet, his mind was numb, and he fumbled a lot. Eithne started to worry that too many nights with her medicines would do more harm than was good for a lad his age.

So that night as the caravan reached Dun Drumkirk, she decided Rhoyd could do without his draught.

The dreams were so bad it took most of the night to calm the men both on and off watch.

That caravan quickly let them go, as did the next one that took them closer to Dun Clachghluin.

It was then Conor looked eastward and decided they would make it a short year and head back for Loughan and Wenthorn now.

My dreams have cost us dearly. They had to sell the pack mare, and for the last sen'night, they had slept on the road more than not. Rhoyd tried to give Conor his own silver--the silver his Aunt Genna was forever sending him to cover the cost of books and paper and ink for his studies--but Conor refused the offer.

"'Tis my duty to take care of ye, lad. Not the other way round. Save yer silver. We'll get by just fine."

How? Rhoyd had thought glumly. His dreams were taking their toll on all of them. They made Conor sullen and Eithne irritable. They quarreled more than usual. And Rhoyd felt miserable because of it.

All my fault, he thought as he turned to look at the marker stone centered in the crossroads. Its face bore carvings of towns and had the names chiseled above the pictures and marks to indicate the number of leagues to each one. The northeasterly side said Faolanwold. Above that was a picture of a wolf behind a tree. Rhoyd frowned and glanced at the other words below it. Heatherbloom, Coldforge, Dun Faolan, Fallonclach. A heather blossom, an anvil, a keep and what looked like a stack of stones were depicted. He stared hard at the latter, for to his mage eyes, it seemed to shimmer. Or was it the shadows and the angle of the sun? The stone itself? He was tempted to ride closer and put a hand on the rough surface to see for himself. But a movement suddenly distracted him.

Conor rode his warhorse Battlebrute to the southeast side of the stone and scowled.

"What's wrong?" Eithne asked.

"Just thinking," Conor said. "We could take the long road through Tamhasg Wood and not go through the mountains. 'Twould be the easier route on the horses."

Eithne looked southeast and frowned. "I'm not so sure that would be a good idea. Are those storm clouds I see?"

Conor glanced southward and hissed, "Horns," under his breath.

Rhoyd saw what she meant. The southeast horizon bore a rim of charcoal clouds. He closed his eyes and with mage senses, he touched the currents of the air. Static fingers tickled him.

There was a storm, a vast one stretching for leagues across the south. Much power and fury filled it. Briefly, he let his senses get caught in the whirling maelstrom. He could have easily let it suck him out of his flesh, drag him through the air like a leaf in a gale. But instead, he pulled away from the power, opened his eyes and sighed.

"Well, lad?" Conor asked.

"She's right. It's a really big storm," Rhoyd said.

Conor grunted. "Well, then I guess it's Faolanwold for us after all."

"You sound displeased to be going that way," Eithne said. "We've crossed through Faolanwold a number of times over the years, and it's never been a problem. And it's still early enough in the year that we won't have to worry about snow in the pass."

"Aye, well, I heard a few rumors," Conor said carefully glancing at Rhoyd.

Did I do something wrong? Rhoyd wondered.

"Rumors?" Eithne said. "Was that what the old farmer was filling your head with this morning?"

"He told me there were ravenous hungry beasts on the prowl," Conor said.

Beasts? Rhoyd shuddered as the harrowing end of his dream tried to creep out of the shadows of his mind.

"What sort of beast?" Rhoyd asked.

Conor offered a reassuring smile. "Probably no more than wolves stealing sheep, lad," he said. "This time of the year, they do hunt to fill their belly for winter, because if it's long and cold, they might nearly be starved in the spring."

"But even hunting packs of wolves rarely bother travelers in autumn," Eithne said. "There is still plenty of natural game. Stoats, hare, deer."

Conor nodded and Rhoyd wondered if there was something he was not saying.

"Like as not," Conor said at length, "that auld farmer was breaking wind. I ne'er thought there was much stool in his tale."

"Conor!" Eithne said and rolled her eyes. "Must you always be so crude?"

Rhoyd smiled. That was more like it.

Conor winked. "Faolanwold it is," he said. "Five days to Dun Faolan by the marker. Let's hope we can get a few good nights' sleep between here and there."

He put heels to Battlebrute's flanks. The warhorse grunted and started on with a kick.

Rhoyd frowned until Eithne rode close on Maudie and leaned over to touch his hand. He started, looking at the concern in her dark eyes. Like Conor's they were underlined with the blue-black semicircles of exhaustion. The sight sent a sinking sensation through him.

"He doesn't hold it against you, lamb," she said in a reassuring way that nearly brought Rhoyd to tears. He bit his tongue rather than give in to the urge. "Maybe I could give you a mild draught tonight, and you could share the big pallet with us. Warm bodies close by might help keep those wolves out of your dreams."

Rhoyd nodded. They might. Then again...

"Come on, ye dawdlers!" Conor called back. "Or we'll

be spending winter in the mountains."

Eithne rolled her eyes again. "We'd best do as he says," she said.

She clucked to Maudie. The mare started forward more sedately. Rhoyd sighed and reined Moonface around so he could follow.

TWO

In Eithne's opinion Heatherbloom was not so much a village as it was a smattering of stone and peat huts that looked as though they had been randomly tossed about and become rooted to the landscape. While she saw no particular arrangement, there were paths leading hither and yon, and all seemed to merge in a central area. There she spied a small pit inset with stones on one side to form a semicircular bench. A pathway of stairs using the natural cut of the earth occupied both ends. A few tables made from wood were scattered about as well. In the middle burned a large bonfire. The lower side sat open and sloped down to a view of the meadow and the stone-studded moors with trees in the distance. Even now, men were gathering about and feeding the flames with pieces of wood as they shared flagons of ale.

No inn, she thought glumly. Like as not, they would be sleeping in someone's barn. Though for the life of her, she saw nothing resembling such a structure anywhere. Indeed, the livestock not penned in small circles of stone were wandering aimlessly through the village, some going in and out of huts. Eithne fought against frowning. While it was not unusual to see livestock sharing quarters with their owners, she was not so sure she liked the thought of waking up with piglets and sheep and chickens walking around her.

She knew better than to say so. Conor would just accuse her of being soft.

He was riding at the head of their small party now, wending his way towards the main area on horseback.

Heads turned and watched their progress as he stopped at the edge and motioned for her and Rhoyd to stay back and mounted. Calmly, Conor dismounted, resting one hand on the hilt of his sword as he walked up to the head of one set of stairs and faced the men now gathering like a pack of hounds scenting a new alpha. She glanced over them, ready to call out at the first sign of danger.

Conor merely nodded respectfully. "Failte!" he called.

From the midst of the gathering, a grizzle-faced man with visible battle scars and a mane of salt and pepper hair stepped forward. He wore a large penannular broach on one shoulder, and the length of his plaidie caught up in a particular style that Conor once told her meant this man was a chief.

"Failte," the older man returned. "Name yourself stranger that you might be welcome here."

"I am Conor MacManahan," Conor replied, and Eithne felt her brows twitch. Conor rarely used the "mac" even in his native country, so there must have been a reason. "This is my wife Eithne who is a True Healer, and that wee lad is our son Rhoyd."

"I'm not wee," Rhoyd muttered to her and Eithne shook her head. She watched two lads creeping around the edge of the crowd who traded glances and gestured towards Rhoyd. Why? Could they see that he was mageborn, or was it his name? The older of the pair stepped forward and whispered something to the grizzled old man. He arched an eyebrow and smiled, though his gaze never wavered from Conor's presence.

"Then come to our fire, you and your family, and be welcome, Conor of the Manahans," the old man said. "I am Angus MacLean, Chief of this clan, and these are my sons Kian and Rory." He gestured to the pair who watched Rhoyd.

"My thanks, Laird MacLean," Conor said. "We seek shelter for the night. Might there be a byre or a sheltering stone about that we could use for this purpose?"

"Nonsense," Angus said. "We do not send visitors to sleep in the cold. It's too dangerous even for the livestock to be left out in the gloaming these days. There is plenty of room for yer family and yer livestock up in my auld mother's croft. She has little need of it, having left for the Summerland."

Dangerous? Eithne frowned. In spite of her curiosity as to what he might mean, she held her tongue.

"I thank ye for yer hospitality then," Conor said. "And I hope yer mother's walk into the Summerland went well by her."

"Her passing, I fear, was not timely in spite of her great age," Angus said with a shake of his head. "She went into the braes to gather herbs and fell to her death. Alas, a wolf got to her corpse before we did."

"I'm sorry to hear that," Conor said with a quick glance at Rhoyd. The lad looked pale. Eithne reached over and touched his hand, and he glanced at her, blue eyes wide.

Conor turned back to the gathering. "I would like to add that in exchange for yer hospitality, if ye have any among yer clan in need of healing, my wife will gladly give freely of her gift."

There were murmurs all around. True Healers were rare in many parts these days. Laird MacLean looked at his men and nodded.

"We accept your offer MacManahan," he said and turned to his sons. "Lads, go and spread the word. If any be weak or ill or infirmed and have need of healing, tell them that we have a True Healer among us this night. And tell the womenfolk not needed to assist her that we would have a feast. Master Dermot, would you do the honor of butchering one of my bull calves for the meat."

The village exploded with a flurry of activity, folks scuttling about and hurrying in different directions. Conor came over and assisted Eithne down from Maudie's back. It was not that she needed his help to dismount, but she knew from experience that he wanted these people to see that she was indeed his wife. A woman unwed in Keltora, he once told her, was a woman thought to be in need of a man unless she was mageborn. A silly custom as far as she was concerned, but she had spent enough years in this part of the world to know better than to argue.

He had hardly released her before a gaggle of village women came forward to greet her with smiles and gestures and chattering. This too, she had learned, was a part of the ritual she found a bit absurd. Long ago, Conor warned her in their travels that the smaller villages of Keltora tended to stick to the "old ways" of separating women and men when it came to tasks. That only the men folk gathered at the fire while the women took themselves elsewhere to spin, sew, cook, and gossip. It was not a lifestyle Eithne could ever bring herself to imitate when they were elsewhere. And Conor knew better than to try to force her to behave this way.

"I didn't marry ye because ye needed a master to order ye about," he once said. "I married ye because my heart told me ye were as strong and fierce as any fighting man, and that ye were a woman not given to fainting and fripperies and gossiping like a fishwife."

For that, she was always grateful. Conor vowed to follow her wherever Diancecht led her in this life, though in truth she noticed her god did little to interfere in most of Conor's plans. She was willing to indulge in this nonsense when they traveled through the remote parts of Keltora.

The women led her to a place where she could settle in and work her healing gifts. They took her straight to the deserted cottage on the outermost edge of the village. Two doors faced her, and she was grateful to see one of them was large enough for horses to enter. She was led through the smaller one into a single chamber walled away and separated from the livestock section. It was clear that no one had been there for at least a moon, for there was a grey gloom to the place. But the women bustled and chatted and set about making the area more presentable. A few younger ones came in carrying water and wood. Another started to build a peat fire in the hearth that occupied one corner of the room. There was a small window near the door and one to the back, and a third that allowed one to check on the livestock.

The cottage was a bit musty smelling as well. At least they have gotten rid of the corpse, she thought gratefully. She had seen that in one village, a body wrapped and resting on a pallet with a patch of green turf on its chest. The smell...she learned that the corpse was that of a man, and that his kin were waiting for one of his sons to return before they buried him. Seven days in the summer made his company unbearable. Even packed with straw and ice as he was, he had rotted.

She refused to stay in that hut. Though she had smelled death often enough on the battlefields of the north, she saw no reason to suffer its odiferous company now.

Eithne was picking a place to set up when Rhoyd suddenly came in carrying her packs with her healing herbs and potions and bandages. The boy looked uneasily about him as the women suddenly rushed him and began to coo at what a handsome lad he was.

"Such eyes," one said. "Blue as summer."

"And such a sweet face," another said. "You just want to kiss him over and over."

Rhoyd opened his mouth to protest as he tried to worm past the wall of women. Eithne wanted to laugh at his plight, but she smiled instead and said, "Thank you, Rhoyd. Bring those here to me, my lad."

He hurried over to her side, looking uncertain.

"Would you like to stay and help me?" she asked, and almost lost her composure when panic took his features. "Or would you rather go sit with Conor and the men?"

Relief filled his eyes. "With Conor," he said, and before any of the women could stop him, he bolted out of the croft like a rabbit pursued by hounds. Only then did she allow herself to laugh a little.

She quickly set out her healing herbs and elixirs, and then turned to the women.

"If you bring in the first patient, I will begin," Eithne said.

The women worked like a well-trained militia as they mustered about. Within moments, there was a line at the door of the cottage. Their collective need filled Eithne like a wave of warmth.

She put aside all thoughts of her own comfort and quickly began to deal with them one at a time.

Angus' words about danger had not escaped Conor's notice. He kept his tongue behind his teeth rather than speak of the lad's nightmares or the rumors he had heard of the road ahead. Better to wait until Rhoyd was away to ask.

Why did it have to be wolves?

Conor kept that thought private as he set Rhoyd to the task of taking care of the horses and giving Eithne her packs of healing goods. Of course, the lad did the latter task first, and as soon as he was out of earshot, Conor turned to the small gathering of men. More ale was being brought. The butcher Dermot was about his work, and the scent of blood wafted down from the end of the village where the deed took place. Conor loosened girths and tethered the horses and worked his way into the crowd of men to reach the laird's side. MacLean held out a jack of ale and offered Conor the stone at his side for a seat. Conor took it obligingly and leaned closer.

"So, what is this danger of which you speak?" he asked.

Angus frowned briefly, glancing at those who were closest before he turned to Conor. "We are not certain," he said in a low voice. "Rumors come to us daily from travelers leaving the Faolanwold. We have heard that there have been sightings around Ben Faolan of the..." He lowered his voice even more. " ...Fearfaolan."

Conor kept his expression stoic. Fearfaolan. The "little wolf men?" He had not heard of them since he was a lad. His auld nurse, who was full of tales of the ancient days, told him that they lived in the age before the Great Cataclysm.

"How can that be?" Conor asked. "I remember the tales and they were said to be a peaceful race before they were sundered from the world in the Great Cataclysm."

"Not all were sundered from the world," Angus said. "And perhaps once they were peaceful, but that was in the days before you or I were in our mother's wombs. I have been hearing these rumors for nearly a moon now that they have been seen around the Faolanwold, and that since they have been spotted, there have been many who died cruelly at the jaws of wolves. Women, livestock and bairns, mostly, though I have heard tales of attacks on men at night when the dark gives the beasts an advantage."

Conor opened his mouth to speak when a thin body squeezed into the space at his side. He looked down to see Rhoyd getting comfortable.

"I thought I told ye to tend to the horses after ye took Eithne her things?" Conor said and pointed to the beasts tethered up on the hill.

Rhoyd rolled his eyes. "I forgot," he said.

"Forgetting is no excuse," Conor said. "Yer to tend the horses if ye want to earn yer winter keep, remember? Else wise, I might forget to tell you a story before bed."

Rhoyd wormed his lips into a frustrated sneer and scrambled away.

Angus chuckled. "Ye could have let him stay. My lads would have taken care of bedding and grooming yer beasts."

"The lad has his chores," Conor said, "and I'll not have him shirk them. Besides, it's best he not hear tales of wolves killing men and women and bairns. He has nightmares about wolves as it is."

Angus nodded knowingly. "Fey born, is he?"

Conor nodded, watching for a sign that this was a bad thing.

"Has he the power?"

"More than some might think good for a lad at his tender age," Conor said. "But he will not be trouble if that is what you fear. He knows when to use the glamorie and when to stay his hand."

"Magic is not trouble," Angus said. "I've a daughter gone to Caer Keltora to be trained. 'Twas more trouble to keep the local lads from fighting over her. They looked at her as hounds look at a fresh bit o' meat."

Conor grinned. "My father used to say that sons were easier for that. No dowries needed."

"Well, she needs none now for by king's law, she is her own woman, just as my late mother was," Angus said, and he doffed his jack at the fire in a salute. "'Twas not easy growing up the son of the village mageborn, I can tell ye."

"I can imagine it was quite a trial," Conor said and grinned. "Ye could ne'er get away with mischief."

Angus grunted in agreement. "So, tell me, where are ye heading that would take ye through the Faolanwold?"

"Back to winter in Loughan," Conor said.

"Loughan? I took ye for a highlander. Yer cut and swagger is all Dun Ferlie."

"I trained at Dun Ferlie before I went to war," Conor said. "But I was born in Seanbrae, the highlands on the sea, as some would say."

"Ah, I thought I kenned the name," Angus said. "So ye've ties to the barony of Seanbrae, do ye?"

"Ye could say that," Conor said, eager to keep from going down that path. His past was his past, and he needed it no more. Bastard son of the Baron he might be, but he had grown up in the militia and was his own man now. Besides, he wanted more news of the dangers. It would not take Rhoyd long to deal with the horses.

"Listen, this danger. Do men truly believe the

Fearfaolan are behind it?"

"Surely ye must have heard the tales," Angus said. "They were not always peaceful. When they lost their lands to the Shadow Lord and his monsters, they took to raiding and stealing and even killing."

"But I understood that it was the Shadow Lord of Dun Faolan who destroyed the Fearfaolan because they dared to stand against him in the times of darkness."

"You've a bard's knowledge then." Angus said. "And so it was always said. And may haps ye will find someone closer to the Faolanwold who can tell ye more. But suffice to say that something has been stalking the moors at night since me mother died. She was a woman who had the sense to avoid danger and yet...I will not forget the look on her face when we found her half-eaten corpse. A look of pure fright, it was. A look that gave strong men the..."

Angus paused and Conor turned to follow the sudden shift in the laird's gaze. Rhoyd was returning, dusting horsehairs off his hands onto his breeches. He strode up to Conor and stopped, and the look was almost challenging.

"That was quick," Conor said. "Are ye sure ye got all the saddle marks off them?"

Rhoyd nodded.

"Did ye use the glamorie?"

"Did you feel it?" Rhoyd asked, looking back at Conor with a gaze that would have wilted the heart of a smaller man.

Conor shook his head, trying not to smile at the lad's impertinence.

"Because I didn't use it," Rhoyd said and frowned. "Do you want me to go away?"

Conor heard Angus chuckle.

"Never," Conor said and patted the stone at his side. "Who will look after me when I'm old and dotter?"

"Eithne said you were already dotter," Rhoyd replied as he quickly reclaimed the space at Conor's side.

Angus nearly choked on his ale. Several of the men laughed.

"That woman needs to learn to bind her tongue," Conor said. "And so do you, lad." With that he wrapped strong arms around Rhoyd and buried wriggling fingers in his ribs. Rhoyd tried to escape to no avail, laughing as he struggled.

"Yield!" Rhoyd said as he gasped for breath.

"Louder," Conor said.

"Yield!" Rhoyd shouted.

"All right, then," Conor said and ceased his torments. The men around them chuckled in amusement, and Conor sighed. Hopefully, there would be time to ask about this prowling beast later once the lad retired.

Assuming he does not awaken us all with his dreams.

Eithne gave Rhoyd a mild draught that night, and he quickly sank under a thick cloud of sleep where his dreams did not roam. But he had not been there long when the sensation of cold fingers suddenly walked down his spine and lurched him awake. He rolled over on his pallet with a startled gasp, sitting up and staring at the shadows of the cottage. Mage eyes quickly adjusted as he cast about with mage senses, seeking the cause of his unease.

A glimmer of moonlight from a waxing orb peered through the window, revealing the chamber. Conor and Eithne still slept on their own pallet. Eithne had suggested Rhoyd share with them this night, but he wanted to be brave and show them he could sleep in his own bed without the dreams. Now, he was uncertain that had been a good idea.

But there is nothing wrong here, he told himself. Still, the sensation that an ethereal hand had touched him would not go away.

You can't keep being a bairn. You've killed demons and vanquished darklings and monsters before.

24

But he could not shake his unease as he searched harder through the shadows of the night.

And then he saw her.

Rhoyd blinked. An old woman squatted before the hearth, tracing a finger through the mound of old ashes and new embers. She paused and raised deep green eyes and gazed at him. Then she gestured, "come here" with her finger.

At first, he was reluctant. He had been spirit led more than once in his life, and it never brought anything but trouble. But she looked so sad when he did not move. She sighed and gestured again, and whispered, "Please."

Cautiously, he pushed his blankets aside and stood. The reeds dug roughly into his bare feet as he crossed the floor and stopped a mere arm's length from her. He could see the stones of the hearth through her thin body. She kept one arm hard across her stomach, and he thought there were dark stains visible around the hand.

"I was once as you are," she said softly, her voice a dry husky sound in his head. "And now I am bound to the dark stones of the earth by my own blood and by my death."

Rhoyd frowned. "Who are you?" he whispered, reluctant to wake the others in case this was another variation on his miserable dreams.

"My name is Brina," she whispered. "My son Angus is chief of this clan, and this was my cottage." She heaved a long, soft sigh.

Rhoyd relaxed a little. She was just a spirit. He squatted beside her, and the gesture made her smile. "You said you were as I am," he said. "Do you mean that you were mageborn?"

"Aye," she said, "though I did not have much power. I came late into mine--too late to stop my father from giving me to the last Laird of Heatherbloom."

Rhoyd nodded. Most mageborn, according to his Aunt Genna who taught him magic in the late winter, came into their powers when twelve summers had passed. "Making our lives doubly hard," she would say. "But some mageborn bloom late, and some not at all, though they can sometimes sense magic in the world. Mage blood tends to run in families, and depending on how strong it was, it could produce several mageborn in a single generation, or none for many."

Rhoyd, however, was practically born to his power. He hardly seemed to be getting older, and there were many things coming to pass he was not certain he was ready to deal with. His late Uncle Fenelon was always telling Rhoyd the mistake was not taking him from his birth home and training him from the time he could make mage lights.

Rhoyd shook those thoughts aside, for they only reminded him how his real mother's death had changed his life forever. Besides, Brina was drawing a finger through the ashes again, and though a very small puff of them moved as though stirred by the faintest of breezes, she made no discernible mark. Her face settled back into a sad frown.

"How did you die?" Rhoyd asked.

She looked furtively over one shoulder at Conor and Eithne, and then leaned closer to Rhoyd. He felt the static of her life essence as a faint wind fluttering small hairs. Like the cold kiss of winter on his skin.

"They would not wish for you to know," she said. "But I will tell you this. Those they blame are not always what they seem. And that which took my life untimely left its mark on me."

She stood up suddenly, turning to face him, moving her arm aside. Though she was but a wisp of smoke and air, he saw the gleam of blood where her stomach lay torn open, and her entrails slithered free. Rhoyd gasped, lurched back, and stumbled in his fright.

"It will seek you out for your blood," she said. "It will know you for who and what you are, Ard Magister."

She stretched her hand towards him as he desperately

scrambled backwards like a crab. Her ethereal hand slipped into his chest as she effortlessly followed, floating above the floor. The touch burned cold inside him and froze him into place."

"You must know it as well," she said.

No! He slapped at her, pushing this way and that, fighting to keep her out of his flesh. But visions stole over him despite his efforts. He saw through her eyes the heather drenched in early morning dew. The sunlight brushing the tips of the braes flamed like watch fires against the dark.

"It must be gathered before the sun touches it," he heard her voice saying as she climbed the hillside. Here and there, the long stones and the predawn angle of the sun made deep blue shadows. She moved among them, carefully picking her way along steep faces and sheer drops until she reached a place that suited her needs. Kneeling, she began to push the heather aside, reaching beneath to glean some treasure he knew nothing about.

Her fingers touched a wall of black stone. The plants had grown over its smooth surface, hiding it from the world and the sun. She tore them away, her curiosity strong, and stopped as her efforts revealed marks of an ancient time. She crouched to find a better angle in the shadows that would allow her to read.

Her foot slipped on the soft spongy ground, throwing her to her knees. To keep from knocking her head against the stone, she flailed with her hands. They struck the surface hard as her balance went askew. Where the marks had been carved out of the smooth surface, the thin edges were like slivers of steel. They sliced into her palms as she continued to drop, leaving a trail of her blood across the surface.

Brina gasped in pain and surprise as she landed on her stomach and scrambled to get up again before she fell over the edge. But she ceased her struggles when she saw the stone drink in her blood like a dry sponge. Before she could regain her feet, it split open like a maw. From that dark sprang a beast with deformed jaws that bit into her, ripping her open as it threw her over the edge and back into the early light of the sun.

"No!" Rhoyd shouted. Those jaws were the same deformed ones that haunted his nightmares. He jerked back again, tripped as he sought to rise and fell into a corner. His fall rocked the shelves there and spilled crockery. A bowl thundered across his shoulder and smashed into the reed-strewn floor, shattering.

"Howt awa!" a familiar voice shouted.

"Blessed Brother!" another cried.

Rhoyd covered his head against the avalanche of crockery that descended and shattered around him. The loud clatter went on for ages, or so it seemed. Then silence fell and only then did Rhoyd uncover his head to stare at the destruction.

Conor and Eithne stood over him as though uncertain what to do or say. Old Brina had vanished. Rhoyd furtively glanced about, seeking her with mage senses and eyes, but saw no sign.

"Well, this is a first, I'll wager," Conor said and cautiously picked his way past broken pots to kneel beside Rhoyd. "Are ye all right, lad? Was it the dream again?"

Rhoyd hesitated then slowly whispered, "It wasn't a dream."

"What?"

"She showed me how she died," Rhoyd said and looked straight into Conor's green eyes.

"Who?" Conor asked.

Rhoyd took a deep breath. "The woman who lived here," he said. "The mother of Laird Angus MacLean. Her spirit was here."

Conor looked solemn as he glanced up at Eithne. She shrugged as he turned back at Rhoyd. "How did she die, lad?" Conor asked.

"It was bound into the stone," Rhoyd said. "But her

blood set it free."

"Yer blethering in riddles, lad," Conor said and picked up one of the few pots that had survived the tumble and smash. "Are ye sure this corrie didn't addle yer pate when it fell on your head?"

Rhoyd took another deep breath. "Her name is Brina and she was one of the mageborn, and that which killed her is the same creature that attacks me in my dreams."

Conor sighed and glanced at Eithne again. "Another draught?" he asked.

"Too soon," she said glancing at all the broken pots and shaking her head.

"I don't need the draught," Rhoyd said. "I'll be fine if..." He hesitated.

"Ye want to sleep with us then, lad?" Conor asked.

Rhoyd nodded. *Stupid bairn! That's what I am.*

Conor reached out and pushed a hand fondly through Rhoyd's hair. "It's all right, lad. I won't think less of ye for it."

"Well, before we go back to bed, I think we should at least pick up this mess out of respect for our host and his late mother." She glanced over her shoulder as though expecting the lady to be standing there, wearing a disapproving scowl. Rhoyd fought a giggle.

"She's not dangerous," he said, even though he knew she had reached into him.

He dutifully began gathering broken bits of pottery and dumping them into the few whole pieces of crockery left. With Conor and Eithne assisting him, the chore was swiftly finished. Then Conor moved over to the hearth and murmured, "'Tis a cauld draft here," as he rebuilt their fire from the embers huddling among the ashes. Flames quickly bloomed under Conor's coaxing, and once that was done, Rhoyd was allowed to crawl into the large pallet with his adopted parents. He coiled up against Conor, relishing the bronze warmth of his aura.

But just before Rhoyd closed his eyes, he glanced once more at the hearth.

Auld Brina was there, crouched on the stones as before, moving her finger through the ashes. Rhoyd closed his eyes, determined to ignore her and go to sleep. He feared that looking into her eyes would make the vision of her death linger in his mind and invade his dreams.

He pressed close to Conor and prayed to all the gods he knew that the rest of the night would be peaceful.

As if to answer, sleep took him deep below the realm of bad dreams.

THREE

Rhoyd was still asleep when Conor awoke the next morning. The lad was snuggled tightly into the crook of Conor's arm, fingers woven into the plaidie serving as an extra blanket when the fire finally died and the dark hours of predawn chilled the air. *Will he ever outgrow that?* Conor wondered as he was forced to rise and leave the woolen lengths of his family tartan with Rhoyd. But Conor felt undressed without its weight, so he snatched up the shorter piece--Eithne's marriage plaidie, which she had given to Rhoyd--and tossed the two double-ells about his shoulders for warmth.

Eithne was already up and about. In the neighboring section of the hut, Conor could hear the restless whuffling of the horses wanting to be fed. He pushed open the rickety cottage door and poked his head out in search of his wife. She stood down in the heart of the village, stretching hands towards the fire that burned in the central pit and talking to Laird MacLean. Her words floated back to Conor on the breeze.

"...And we must apologize for the broken crockery, and if you will but tell us the worth, we would gladly make amends..."

Horns, Conor thought and wrinkled his nose. So, his wife was trying to buy peace? He'd best get out there before she gave away her mare or his warhorse. These highlanders had no use for coins, but plenty for livestock and goods. No good would come of that.

Since highlander cottages tended to have small doors--easier to defend when hordes of raiders came a' calling--Conor had to duck to keep from banging his forehead on

31

the low lintel. And naturally, since there was a step up to negotiate as well, he was looking at the ground to make certain he did not misstep on the threshold. But he paused when his gaze dropped to the ground. It had rained in the night, and scattered reeds were embedded in the muck where they had softened and sunk. He could see footprints to one side of the door, no larger than those of a child. Odd. The lad had not been out in the night. Of that, Conor was certain. Besides, these footsteps took a strange path. They walked up to the side of the door, and then wandered over to the window before trailing away.

Someone else's child, he thought and hauled himself out of the cottage, rapidly crossing the ground to join Eithne at the pit.

"And I can assure you, Mistress MacManahan, that there is no need," Angus said. "Ye have done more than enough cures last evening to make up for the loss of a hundred pots."

That's a relief. Conor slowed his pace.

"And anyway," Angus went on, "my mother was one of the mageborn, and some said she were as auld as the braes. She had more crockery than a good woman needs in a single lifetime."

Conor chuckled, and Eithne cast a stern look in his direction. Clearly, she was not as amused by the laird's wit. Angus took one look at Conor and grinned.

"Yer plaidie's a bit shorter this morning. Did it shrink in the night?"

"This belongs to the lad," Conor said. "He's wrapped in mine like it was a cocoon. And anyway, he only broke half the pots in the corner."

"When my mother was laid in her cairn, we broke dozens and scattered the shards on her grave."

"That seems a waste of pots," Eithne said.

"Old custom, woman," Conor said. "Keeps animals from digging up the remains before the ground has settled and firmed up." He decided not to mention that it was also believed that the broken bits would serve to keep the dead from walking, though from what Rhoyd said last night, that clearly didn't matter with mageborn.

Eithne raised eyebrows and nodded.

"Besides," Angus said. "None here that wants what was once me mother's. There's many in these parts who believe that her possessions will be haunted because she died before her time."

"Oh, surely not," Eithne said, but she glanced quizzically at Conor as she spoke.

She's remembering what the lad said about being shown the old woman's death.

"'Tis True," Angus said. "All know that a mageborn what dies before their time will come back to haunt their home. As it is, my eldest is about to wed a young lass from Doonahill Croft, and he and his bride-to-be have refused to accept my mother's cottage as a bridal gift. My sons may not have been born with their sister and grandmother's gifts, but they have the sense of magic on them. They say they have felt my mother about the village."

"How long since she died?" Conor asked.

"Just over a moon now," Angus replied.

A moon? Conor thought, again reminded of how long it had been since Rhoyd began to dream...and how long since the deaths started around the Faolanwold.

"Yer more than welcome to use the place another night," Angus said. "We'll be pulling it doon and scattering the stones come the next moon. The rest of the village won't rest easy until we do."

"Another night?" Conor said. "One was all we asked." He glanced at Eithne.

"Actually, I asked to stay another night," she said. Conor started to protest that she was wrong. "Master Dermot's wife is about to birth her first, and she is not having a good time bearing the child, I thought it would be best. Her water broke this morning, and I felt her need..."

"All right, all right," Conor said and waved his hands to stop her from going into any more detail. While he had been there for the birth of his own child, he preferred not to share the matter of other women's pangs. "Another night it is, woman."

"Dermot will be grateful," Angus said.

Conor nodded. *Well, another night canna hurt, can it?* It would give the lad another good night of sleeping under a more welcoming roof.

"And since ye are staying, would ye care to join us on the hunt?" Angus said. "Both you and yer lad are welcome."

"What game are we hunting?" Conor asked.

"Someone stole a pair of auld Tam's laying hens in the night, and he wants to catch the thief."

"We're hunting a fox then?" Conor said.

"Not unless this one walks on two legs," Angus said and laughed.

"Why didn't he hear the thief?" Eithne asked. "Hens become notoriously noisy when they are being stolen out of their roosts."

Angus looked perturbed. "Aye well, 'twas only two, and if the thief were quick enough to snap their necks, they would have gone quietly enough."

Eithne arched her eyebrow at such a sharp angle Conor knew what was going through her thoughts. These folks had their livestock indoors at night to protect the beasts from wild animals. How could the thief enter the shelter of their roof while they slept without being heard?

But then he thought of the small tracks outside their own window. "I'll fetch the lad," Conor said. "Best to give him time to wake up. He's a bit of a wee bear in the mornings."

Angus chuckled as though amused by this. "We'll wait for ye, then," he said and started off in another direction.

Turning, Conor started back up the hill to the cottage and stopped to look again. The tracks going away certainly went up into the rocks and the braes that rose over Heatherbloom. Conor followed them down towards the cottages. They came from one of the lower structures. Just outside the livestock entrance, several men gathered. One was a rusty old codger who flapped his arms like an agitated rooster. Auld Tam, I'll wager.

The chicken thief had wandered up to see if there was anything worth pilfering in the old woman's cottage and finding it occupied, had gone away.

Conor frowned. There was a bogie feel to all this that he did not like.

Best wake the lad, then, and see about finding this thief.

He turned once more and started back up the hill to the old woman's cottage.

"A hunt?" Rhoyd said as he pushed his hair back out of his eyes so he could see to lace his boots. "What sort of hunt?"

He hoped Conor did not hear the reluctance in his voice. Rhoyd had never really been fond of killing animals for sport. Oh, he understood when game was killed for food, and he had helped Conor clean rabbits often enough to be inured to the idea of preparing meat. But to hunt solely for the purpose of pitting yourself against some animal in the forest or the fields, that seemed so unnecessary and even dangerous to the balance of nature.

"For a thief," Conor said.

Having rousted Rhoyd from the bed, Conor had reclaimed his own plaidie, folding, wrapping and belting it around him in a manner that always fascinated Rhoyd to witness. Now Conor sat in the one sturdy chair this cottage had to offer, leaning back, and bracing his feet on the table as he cleaned his sword.

"A thief?" Rhoyd said, and having finished with his lacings, he stood up. "What was stolen?"

"A couple of laying hens, though I seriously doubt we'll

be bringing them back," Conor said. His attention was on the edge of his blade. He studied it and nodded in satisfaction.

Rhoyd frowned. There were tiny nicks in the steel, visible to mage eyes trained by a smith, though they were too small to matter now. He didn't mention them as he settled into the other chair, which was more rickety and uneven.

"Then why are they bothering?" he asked.

"Bothering?" Conor asked and sheathed his sword.

"To go after the hens," Rhoyd said plainly. "If they have already been eaten..."

"It's the thief they want, lad," Conor said and briefly frowned in thought. "These highlanders live close to the land and have little enough for themselves. They're generous to their guests, their neighbors, and their friends--even to strangers when it suits them, but thieves are not to be tolerated. Besides, A bit of hill walking will make ye sleep like a stone tonight."

"So, we're staying here another night?" Rhoyd ventured. He laid one hand on the table and leaned against the edge.

"Aye, the woman's got one here that's about to pop another mouth to feed, so we're to stay here another night. Does that worry ye?"

Rhoyd quickly shook his head, but he glanced at the hearth as he did. Brina was nowhere to be seen, though he sensed some lingering part of her infusing the air of the cottage. What was it his late Uncle Fenelon had once said? One law bound all spirits not crossing to the Summerland. They had to return to their graves at cock's crow.

He wondered where Brina was buried.

A large finger tapped the top of his wrist, startling him. He glanced up to find Conor leaning over the table, wearing a look of concern.

"What are ye not saying, lad?" Conor asked. Rhoyd

started to refute the claim. "And don't tell me nothing," Conor added. "I know that look as sure as I know the weft and weave of my own plaidie. Something is troubling ye."

Rhoyd sighed and glanced back at the hearth. "She was here all-night last night," he said.

"She?" Conor asked.

Glancing back, Rhoyd replied, "The old woman Brina. She told me that her blood brought it out of the black stone. And those who would be blamed for her death were not at fault. Who are they blaming for her death?"

Conor cocked an eyebrow at an angle. "It's just an old myth, and I'm not so certain I believe them. But when men feel fear for something they cannot see, they often turn to stories to make their fears go away."

"What stories?" Rhoyd asked, unable to hide his sudden interest.

Conor smiled and leaned back in the chair again.

"Well, now, I canna say as I know the whole tale, lad," he said. "But 'twas told to me when I was a lad that these lands on which we stand once belonged to the Seelie folk known as the Fearfaolan."

"The little wolf men?" Rhoyd said and frowned.

"Ye know the tale?" Conor asked.

"I know the words," Rhoyd said, and Conor nodded.

"Aye, that is what their name means. And it is from the old tongue that was spoken before men ruled the lands and the Old Ones still walked among us. But the Fearfaolan lived when dark times covered the world, some say before the Great Cataclysm."

"The Age of the Shadow Lords," Rhoyd said.

"Are ye sure ye don't already know this story?" Conor asked with a teasing grin.

"Uncle Fenelon was always telling me about the Shadow Lords when Aunt Genna couldn't hear him," Rhoyd said. "And anyway, I defeated one once...sort of. Remember?"

"Aye," Conor said. "I remember that all too well. Ye forced him right back into his tomb, ye did. Ye were a brave lad to face something so dreadful. Just like when you faced that thing called the Venomous Dark."

The words "brave lad" sent a delicious shiver racing through Rhoyd. He had never counted himself brave before then. Even when he faced the Venemous Dark, he didn't really feel all that brave.

But his moment of triumph was interrupted when a heavy fist knocked on the cottage door, nearly shoving it inward. "MacManahan, are ye and yer son ready?" Angus called from outside.

"As we'll ever be," Conor said. He stood up and strapped on his sword.

Rhoyd hopped up and snagged his own plaidie and opened the door when Conor gestured that he should do so. Several men, including Angus and his eldest son Rory, stood waiting on the patch of ground rolling down from Brina's cottage. They had bows, staffs and long dirks at the ready. *Like a small army heading to war,* Rhoyd thought and fought a shudder.

One of the men was straining to hold back a large hound on a lead of rope. The shaggy-coated beast pulled against its burly master's grip and whined as it sniffed the ground near the small window.

"Turi's dog has a good whiff o' the thief," Angus said. "The scent is still fresh enough because of the rain last night. Let's make haste before they reach the Falls of Dubhran."

Conor urged Rhoyd out of the hut and closed the door in their wake. Turi let his hound have a bit more lead, and snuffling, the dog leapt forward. They took off, letting the hound lead the way. Rhoyd was forced to nearly run to keep up with the men and Conor as they surged up the hillside towards the rocky high ground.

I could never be a highlander, Rhoyd thought. It wasn't long before he felt his lungs struggle for air and a stitch in his side. Midday saw them reaching a summit, barely stopping for a break. Fortunately, as the terrain grew steep even the men had to slow their long strides. This allowed Rhoyd to tag along with the men who were clearly not up to this exercise.

Turi's hound suddenly stopped and sniffed the ground and whined in confusion. They had reached a place where rills of water trickled across the face of some larger stones. Moisture lay heavy on the air. Somewhere beyond the growing veil of mist that capped the higher places, Rhoyd heard the rush and roar of a waterfall.

The trail twisted more now, running in and out among great stacks of giant boulders and rocks.

"Horns," Angus said bitterly. "It's gone aground."

"But where," his son Rory said, gesturing around them. "There be no place here to hide more than a wee fox."

"Maybe they climbed up the rocks and got on the path above?" another suggested.

"'Tis possible," Angus agreed. "Turi, take the dog up and around and see if he picks up the scent on the higher trail."

Rhoyd had barely caught up when the rest of the men swiftly moved on. Frowning, he gave up all hope of sitting down to rest. Conor would probably have a fit if Rhoyd fell too far behind. He sighed and started to take another step. And paused.

The men moved on, but Rhoyd held his place and glanced towards the break in the rocks. A bit of wind was stirring and bringing a scent. Was it a cave? He shifted a step, then another and saw that the stones overlapped, and the angle of the shadows hid what lay behind. An opening that someone not much larger than himself could slip into. Issuing from the depths, he heard the faint phitta-phip-phitta-phip of a rapidly beating heart.

Cautiously, Rhoyd stepped closer, giving mage eyes time to adjust to the shadows filling those depths. The odors of moist earth and fowl and musk mingled in his nose as he peered deeper into the hole. At his feet, he made out a scattering of chicken feathers. Then a shape manifested, just the faintest outline, a hooded figure crouched against the back wall, clutching two nearly naked hens to its chest. Rhoyd froze and stretched mage senses like fingers to test the "thing."

It flinched, and he heard a whimper of panic much like the whine of a trapped dog. Just as Rhoyd thought of shouting for others, he heard Conor call.

"Rhoyd!"

The shout of his own name distracted him so that he glanced briefly over one shoulder. That was all the distraction the thief needed. Just as Rhoyd looked back, the figure rushed him, swinging the chickens like small sacks. One slick meaty body slammed into Rhoyd's face as someone his own size shouldered him abruptly and thrust him out of the cave.

He tumbled back and fell, hitting something hard. Pain lanced his skull, and his senses were bludgeoned with confusion. But someone small as himself came running out of the cave into the light and paused.

"Horns, what in the name of Cernunnos?"

Conor? Through pain-blurred eyes, Rhoyd saw a fox's head peering from under the hood before it turned and fled. Moments later, a foot thumped on the turf near him as he struggled to rise, but no part of his body would cooperate with the pain in his head.

"Howt awa," Conor muttered. "Easy, lad, yer bleeding."

Bleeding and passing out, Rhoyd thought before the darkness swept over him.

Dermot's wife Sioban was a tiny woman, and her belly full of child made her look so much smaller to Eithne. *She can't be more than a child herself,* Eithne thought as she studied those vixen-like features drenched in sweat. Sioban's eyes reminded Eithne of a fox, for they were brown with a hint of gold, and her hair now plastered like a tight cowl about her eldritch face was the color of amber rarely seen even among Keltorans who were famous for spawning so many with red hair. Sioban's small size worried Eithne now.

"Just how old are you?" Eithne asked as she helped ease Sioban into the birthing chair that the two women assisting her had carried into Dermot's cottage earlier. Dermot himself stood just outside the cottage door, shifting back and forth like an impatient horse, his brow continually furrowed with a frown.

"She's four and twenty," he called in before Sioban could reply.

Eithne looked incredulous at this. The tiny woman merely nodded as she grimaced in pain. Her water broke long before the men headed out on the hunt earlier this morning, and now that midday had passed, Sioban's pains were coming closer and closer together, leaving Eithne with no doubt that the birthing would be soon.

"Then you have discovered some secret of eternal youth, my dear, for which many women would envy you," Eithne said with a reassuring smile. She pulled the midwife's stool into position. The two women from the village were arranging fresh drying towels and carrying up water to boil.

"It's her blood," Dermot called through the door again. "All her kin were small folk."

As tempting as it was to tell Dermot to go away, Eithne did not. Sioban had already made it clear that she wanted her husband close when her time came. Why, Eithne could not fathom. Most men, in her experience were quite useless when women were giving birth, and it was best to keep them out of the way. *But Conor was at my side when I gave birth to our son Taran.* He had held her hand and was there for her when the ordeal nearly proved too much for her own small body. She could not deny Dermot his rights as a father, not in a land where such traditions were held strong.

So Eithne gestured for the spare stool to be placed to the side of the birthing chair. "Master Dermot, will you

41

come in and sit down now?" she said.

He thundered through the door like a large puppy and claimed the seat. Then he took his wife's small hand in his own large one and squeezed it with such tenderness, all Eithne's misgivings faded.

"I will be plain with both of you," Eithne said as she arranged all to her liking. "Your child is quite large, and its birth will certainly be painful to you. What I fear is that its passage may be dangerous as well. I prefer to let nature take its own course in these matters, but if worse comes to worse, I would not hesitate--assuming you are willing--to remove it by more drastic means. But I must have your consent."

Sioban blinked and glanced at Dermot who nodded. She glanced back at Eithne. "Do what must be done, Mistress MacManahan," she said quietly. "I wish above all that my child should live."

"Then I will do what I can," Eithne said. "With the Brother's help, I will do all I can."

She slipped her hands under the birthing shift, lifting the thin fabric and running her hands skillfully over Sioban's belly. To Eithne's relief, the head and heels felt as though they were in the right position. *That is a good sign,* she thought.

"So, all of your kin are small folk," Eithne said, hoping the light chatter would ease the new mother's tension. "Are you not from this village then?"

The question made Sioban tense even more. Dermot leaned towards Eithne as though to confide in her. He wore a troubled frown, and his bushy brows formed a single line of worry.

"My wife is from a land far away," he said as though the subject were not one to his liking.

Eithne could not miss the move when the two women who assisted her traded looks and smirked knowingly.

"Far Away?" one whispered. "Is that the name of the village now?"

"And here I thought she came from the heart of the Faolanwold," the other whispered back. "She is small enough to be one of the..."

"Enough!" Dermot roared and charged to his feet, and the two women froze. "Keep yer wagging tongues still behind yer teeth!"

"Dermot, don't," Sioban said through teeth gritted with pain. "You know it does not matter what they say."

He held his place, and Eithne worried that he might throw himself at the pair like a rabid dog. But Sioban reached over and put a hand on his knotted fist ever so tenderly.

"Please," she said. "I need you here, my husband. Do not give the good healer a reason to send you away."

Slowly, Dermot reclaimed his place on the stool and took his tiny wife's hand, cupping it and bringing it to his lips.

"Beg pardon, Mistress Healer," he said without looking at Eithne. "I have no love of idle gossiping."

"Neither do I," Eithne said, and cast a scolding glance at the pair as they whispered between them. "If you two are to assist me, then I suggest you cease your useless prattle and do as I bid. You fetch more water from the well and set it to boiling in the pit. And you..." She glanced sharply at the second of the pair. "I may have need of a length of clean sinew. If you know where some may be found, you may go fetch it for me now, and if it not clean, make sure you boil it. Go, and don't dawdle."

Both women hurried out of the cottage, looking properly cowed.

"Now, Master Dermot," Eithne said. "You were saying."

She looked at him as Sioban hissed in pain and tightened her grasp. He was distracted briefly until her grip relaxed. Then he sighed.

"It is true, my wife is not from here, and no, she is not what she seems," he said. "But I will not have her true nature known to the likes of..."

"What is her true nature?" Eithne said. "And let me

assure you, that I will say nothing to anyone. But if I am to help your wife through this birthing, I must know."

He nodded, though his eyes held a look of reluctance. "Her mother was a half-blood from the Faolanwold. My wife is actually twice my own age."

"Half-blood?" Eithne said and glanced at Sioban whose eyes suddenly looked ancient.

"My mother was born of a mortal woman and a Seelie man," Sioban whispered. "There are those who say that my grandfather was one of the Fearfaolan."

"Fearfaolan? What is that?" Eithne asked, unable to hide her puzzlement.

"They are an ancient race that once filled this land," Dermot explained. "Some say they are half wolf. Others say they are the children of the Old Ones who were said to have cavorted with animals at times. Still others would have it that they were a people cursed by the gods."

"My father did not know that my mother was a half-blood when he wed her," Sioban said panting, "though I am certain he found out on their wedding night. He feared his neighbors would not be understanding of my mother's nature, so he took her and fled to Coldforge to live for a time. I grew up there knowing that we were different, and that I could not let others know. But when I was nearly grown, my father met his death upon the moor. Another tried to claim my mother as his wife, and when she refused, he tried to take her by force. And in doing so, he found the mark of my kind on her."

"The mark?" Eithne asked.

Sioban stiffened, as her pains grew sharper. Eithne glanced at Dermot for an answer. He frowned. "My wife's mother had fur down her back, much like the pelt of a fox," he said. "My wife also bears this mark, and if any were to find out..."

Eithne nodded. "Your secret is safe with me," she said. "Sioban, I want you to push when I tell you. Dermot, support her and keep her breathing."

He nodded. Sioban was tightening every muscle in her tiny frame, pushing against the babe. The strain turned her pale face a rich shade of plum as she strained to bring her child into the world. Eithne and Dermot both spoke words of encouragement and instruction, and all the while, Eithne whispered under her breath for Diancecht to give this child and the mother his protection.

"Push, push, deep breaths, relax."

She repeated the litany over and over, and with each moment of straining Sioban seemed to grow smaller and smaller. Eithne began to fear that she would have to take the child by forcible means, and she dreaded that, for though with her healing gift, she could staunch bleeding and save lives, if the woman's heart should stop--if she should bleed to death--there would be naught even Eithne could do.

"Push, push." Eithne took a deep breath. Sioban was in tears, and her efforts were weakening. Eithne's hand slid towards the small knife on the bench.

But Sioban suddenly screamed, and the sound reminded Eithne of a she-wolf crying for its cubs. Sioban leaned forward and pushed again, and nature took its course. Her frail body gave a mighty heave, and Eithne suddenly found herself gathering wet, gangling long limbs as the babe slid free like a selkie shedding its pelt. Nearly all arms and legs, and skinny as a twig, the baby came into the world. Eithne quickly cleared the mouth and throat with her finger. She had hardly cleared the birthing matter when healthy new lungs let out a howling squall to equal its mother's cry. Eithne quickly severed the cord and wrapped the babe in the nearest bit of clean linen she could find.

"Is it a son?" Dermot asked, leaning over to peek at the squirming bundle.

By the Brother, the child was like a wild thing, ready to leap out of Eithne's arms.

"Yes," she said and laughed. "It is a son, Master Dermot."

Dermot whooped with joy and charged off his stool, dancing around the cottage like a madman. The two women came hustling back into the cottage, and he grabbed them together, dragging them into a twirl in a space that afforded little such room. Then laughing, he released them, nearly tumbling them to the floor as he leaned over and kissed his sweaty wife.

"A son, did ye hear that, my love. A son!" he said.

Sioban laughed weakly. Dermot turned, pulled out his dagger, and slashed two double ells from his plaidie. "A son to carry on my name," he said. He walked towards Eithne as he held out his hands with the cloth draped across them. "Let me have him."

Eithne knew that she could do no more than submit this poor bairn to his large boisterous father. This was one tradition even Conor assured her she could not deny a man. The first son was always treated to display, wrapped in part of its father's plaidie. She sighed and started to hand the child over when her hand brushed the nape of his neck. In her rush to wrap it and sever the cord, she had failed to notice what her hand now discovered--a patch of wet fur, much like the pelt of a dog.

"Here," one of the women said. "Before ye go carting him about like a sack of tatties, at least let us clean him first."

Eithne froze, meeting Dermot's cheerful gaze, and her look must have been as transparent as water. His eyebrows arched briefly.

"Is he?" Dermot whispered.

"He's just fine," Eithne said with a forced smile and brushed the child's neck against the father's hands. "Come, I shall clean him for you. You see to your wife. And then you can take him out and show him to the rest of the village." She turned to the women. "You two fetch fresh linens for the bed and clean up and bury the afterbirth."

They looked puzzled but showed the good sense to

obey. As they bustled about Dermot nodded and went to assist Sioban from the chair and into the warm bath the women had prepared.

Eithne worked swiftly, washing the blood and mucus away. Her efforts revealed a clean-limbed child with his mother's vixen-like features and a thin dark stripe of fur down his back. The babe continued to wail and squirm lustily as she got it dried and wrapped in linen and plaidie. By the time she was finished, Dermot had managed to divest his wife of her sweaty, blood-soaked birthing gown and into a warm clean one. The women finished the bed just in time. Dermot placed Sioban there and stood up, looking pleased as Eithne offered him his new son.

As if by magic, or perhaps because the baby knew its father's touch, the child ceased to cry. Dermot grinned broadly as he took his son and raised the lad high. Stepping out of the cottage, Dermot shouted, "Come and see the son beget from the lusty loins of Dermot MacDermot."

Dermot MacDermot? Oh dear. Will he call his son Dermot MacDermot MacDermot? Eithne fought the urge to laugh as she checked on Sioban. The woman's tiny face was even paler than before, and she looked exhausted, but her smile of triumph brought warmth to Eithne's heart.

Blessed Brother, thank you for this moment. Thank you for allowing this child and its mother to live...

Need suddenly rushed over Eithne in an icy wave. She caught her breath in surprise and glanced at Sioban, but the tiny woman was not the source. In fact, the need was drawing Eithne to a place outside this house.

Eithne quickly fled the cottage. The remaining villagers, mostly women, elderly, and young children, were gathering to congratulate the new father on his good fortune. She scanned them with a glance, and still could not find the source of need in their midst.

Blessed Brother, what...?

Mist undulated about the higher ground and down in the deeper crevices of this glen. In its grey wisps uphill, she saw movement. A tall man walked at the head of a party of men, his length of plaidie fluttering in the wind.

Conor?

The need came not from him, but from the plaid-wrapped bundle he carried in his arms. A thicket of black hair and boots were all she could see.

"Rhoyd?" she said, panic surging through her as she realized those limbs dangled loose. "Rhoyd?"

She charged up the hill, pushing newcomers out of her way until she reached Conor's side. He looked fairly exhausted himself, and his green eyes carried a hint of his weariness.

"What happened? Is he...?"

"He fell," Conor said softly. "Missed his step, like as not, backing away."

"Quick, let's take him inside," she said, sensing that there was something more here that Conor was not willing to say with so many around.

Conor carried Rhoyd into the cottage and laid the lad on his pallet. Eithne pushed back the plaidie, checking limbs. Nothing was broken, but there was a wound near the base of his skull leaking a little blood.

"Water," she said.

Conor fetched water for her without a word. He stayed just out of the way as she skillfully cleaned the wound. Clearly, it was the sort of ragged damage that occurred when one hit one's head on a stone. *At least Rhoyd is unconscious and will not feel this,* she thought as she quickly stitched the edges together. She looked up to see Conor grimacing worriedly.

"How bad is it?" he asked.

"He'll be fine," she said as she placed one hand on the stitches and the other on Rhoyd's spine. The depth of his need continued to call out to her, filling her with its startled pain. What had he been doing when this

48

happened? She had no time to wonder.

"Blessed Brother, hear my plea." She chanted her prayer and felt Diancecht's power rising in her, warm and reassuring as summer rain. The wound under her fingers was sealed and lost its darkest bruises, leaving the length of a fresh pink scar and pale yellowish patches crisscrossed by threads to indicate that there had been anything at all.

Rhoyd stirred and tried to sit up with a moan.

"Rest, lamb," she said. "You need to rest. I will remove the stitches in the morning. You sleep."

He did not argue but laid the side of his head down on his pillow and closed his eyes. She sighed, packing her sinew and needles away as she looked at Conor.

"What happened to him?" she asked.

"He fell behind," Conor said stiffly. "When I went back to find him, he was on the ground and the chicken thief was disappearing back into the mist. Whether he fell on his own or because he was pushed, I cannot truly say."

"She hit me with a chicken," Rhoyd muttered from the depths of his pillow.

Eithne turned towards the lad.

"She?" Conor said, looking as though he was trying not to laugh aloud. "How can ye certain it was she?"

"I saw her face," Rhoyd muttered. "It was she, even if she did have the face of a fox..."

His words faded under sleep.

"The face of a fox?" Eithne repeated. "What does he mean by that? Just what was this thief? Why didn't you tell the others?"

Conor sighed. "She looked to be no more than a child," he said. "And anyway, I said nothing to the other men because I canna be certain of what I saw, though as he said, it had a fox's face. Besides, I thought it more important to bring the lad straight back. What else would ye have me do, woman? Risk his life to chase a bogie?"

Eithne closed her eyes. "I'm sorry. That is not what I meant. It's just I am very tired after birthing Dermot

MacDermot's son." She took a deep breath and leaned wearily against Conor's shoulder when he moved over beside her.

"Dermot has a son?" Conor said. "Good health to him."

"He is quite the happy man," Eithne said. "I am so tired now. It is not even evening yet, and if I am not mistaken, someone out there is playing pipes."

Conor's arm slid around her, warm and comforting. "'Tis no wonder," he said. "With all the work ye did last night, and now birthing a new Dermot MacDermot ...MacDermot." Eithne laughed out loud then. "Neither of us has gotten as much sleep as we need," he added.

And that is at the heart of it, she thought. Rhoyd's nightmares were taking a toll on them.

If only we could find out why he has these dreams.

"Why don't ye lie down," Conor said. "I've a mind to go sit with the men a while. Sounds like they're starting a ceilidh to herald the new MacDermot's birth."

Eithne smiled. "That would be lovely," she said. Conor kissed her and then coaxed her over to the bed. She crawled into their pallet, lying back on the pillow, and looking up at him. "Just do me one favor," she said.

"Name it," he said.

"Don't dig out your pipes and add to that miserable sound."

"That's no way to talk about highland music," he said.

"It would sound better if it were somewhere else in the highlands, I am certain."

Conor sneered and picked up a pillow, pretending to push it into her face. But he laid it on her chest instead and leaned down to kiss her once more. Then crawling to his feet, he headed for the door.

Within moments, Eithne was asleep.

FOUR

"...And so the midwife says, 'Ian, Ian, bring back the light,' and as soon as he does, out pops another bairn. Well, that makes four now, and Ian thinks it must be the last of them, and he starts to walk away, only to have the midwife shout, 'Ian, Ian, bring back the light.' But Ian, he stops outside the cottage and shouts back, 'Oh, no, Mistress, not this time. I think it's the light that's attracting them...'"

Warm laughter floated up from the fire as Conor made his way back down to where the men were gathered to celebrate the birth of Dermot's son. With it, the sweet music of pipe and whistle careening through the afternoon light where a flurry of dancers leapt and cavorted among the cottages. Ah, new life, how it brought out the best in men. And the worst in women, he thought. Birthing was never a pleasant business for them, and so they often could not understand a man's joy at knowing he had a son and heir to carry on his name. Still, Keltorans carried that tradition with them, no matter where they roamed.

Conor counted himself fortunate that when his own son was born, Eithne had allowed Conor to have his way and bless the child and wrap it in the rent off double ells of his plaidie.

"Honor your firstborn," he remembered his own father once saying to a cousin whose wife had blessed that cousin with a son. "For he may be all you have left to tell the world who you once were as a man."

Conor had never quite understood that until Taran was born. Too bad the pain of it proved all too sharp and bitter when Taran was lost. But the gods had taken pity on Conor and given him another son, and this one might not be blood of his blood or seed of his loins, but he had come to love the lad as his own get and had vowed no man would ever sunder that connection with anything less than Conor's death.

"So how is yer lad?" Angus suddenly asked, and Conor realized that he had taken himself to the heart of the celeidh and claimed his place at the laird's side without so much as a word. He smiled as someone offered him a bowl of reheated stew from last night along with a chunk of white cheese and some brown bread, and a mug of heather ale. Nodding his gratitude to them, he turned to Angus.

"Fine," Conor said. "The woman fixed his head and said he would be as right as rain tomorrow."

"And ye'll be on yer way?" Angus asked.

"Aye," Conor said and dipped part of the bread in the juices and began to eat. He had not realized how hungry he was until he began to devour the fare. Juice dribbled down his chin and he leaned over to catch it with the bowl.

"Well, then, may yer travels be blessed with good fortune, and may the wind stay at your back and the road clear."

"I'll drink to that," Conor said and tossed back a slug of the ale to wash down the mouthful of good meat and bread.

Angus grinned and looked aside.

"...Oh, I know that old tale," someone was saying. "Auld Tam loves his hens more than his wife, and so she threatened to push a hardboiled egg up his arse so he could be more like them..."

Conor grimaced and realized that Angus was staring up at him once more. "So ye did not see the thief when ye found yer son down?" he suddenly asked.

Conor froze, trying to remember if he had said so to

any but Eithne. "I thought I saw someone flitting into the rocks and the mist," he said carefully. "Looked like no more than a child. Might have been a hob, for all I know."

Angus nodded. "I rather thought that wee cave had the look of a hob hole. Might have been the stink of a hob that threw the dog off the thief's scent."

"May haps the thief was a hob," Conor suggested. But he remembered the tracks by the cottage. Hobs did not wear soft-soled boots even in the highlands.

Angus shook his head. "No hob can work a latch that well. Auld Tam lives in terror of his hens getting out as much as he worries about thieves getting in. The draw rope for the bar that locks his barn door is inside Tam's cottage."

Inside? Conor thought. "So, the thief had to enter his cottage to open the hen house?"

"Aye, and that's what has Auld Tam all a' blether. That the thief got in unheard. Mind you, them what has the cottage to either side will tell ye Auld Tam saws iron kettles at night. There could have been an army in his cottage, and I doubt he would have heard it. Deaf as a post, he is."

Auld Tam sat close by, but he apparently did not hear the jibe that started the men around him chuckling merrily.

Conor smiled. The music was growing randy, and he wished he had pulled out his own pipes to join the festivities. But he reminded himself that Eithne had packed the pipes deep after they sold the pack mare.

"When ye reach Coldforge," Angus suddenly said, drawing Conor's attention back, "ask for Whelan MacFee and tell him I sent ye. He's a smith in those parts and a cousin to my clan kin. He'll give ye shelter for the night."

"I shall do that," Conor said as he finished the last of his meal. "My thanks."

"He'll be a good one for gossip of the road too," Angus added. "He'll know if there is danger ye might want to avoid."

A little late for that, Conor thought as he lifted his ale to take another sip. His gaze drifted to the world around them growing dim with the gloaming.

Mist has settled on the higher reaches above the village. Below the peaks of the bens that held court around this glen, patches of fog danced and swirled in the wind like ghosts. Deeper in the glen where there were small hummocks and rolling heather, mist was thickening close to the ground.

But Conor's eyes were drawn from these beauties of his native land to shadows that flitted cautiously among the scattering of stone ranging about like an army from ancient times, littering the rolls and heaves of heather with their grey forms. Shadows that stayed low and moved too swiftly to be men.

"Angus," Conor said. "Look to the lea to yer left, down among the stones, and tell me what ye see."

Angus had been about to take a long quaff of ale. Arching his eyebrows at a quizzical angle, he turned to look down at the glen. A frown furrowed the already deep crevices of his face.

"Horns, those look like wolves," he muttered and rose to his feet.

Conor stood as well. The angle afforded him a better view.

The shadows were wolves, and they appeared to be racing towards the village itself. But why? Men and fire usually kept wolves at bay, but these were forming ranks and advancing with a purpose against their nature.

Angus muttered "Howt awa," and deserted the bench with more agility than Conor would have credited to a man his age. He hurried towards the fire, seizing up one of the limbs and brandishing it like a torch. "Light the watch fires!" he ordered. "Board the livestock and the bairns. There are wolves coming."

Conor was glad to see that not a man among them questioned Angus' word. With the precision of a well-trained militia, men leapt to the chore of gathering branches from the main fire and lighting smaller ones. Women swiftly gathered their bairns, their sheep, cattle and hens, and herded them into the cottages closest at hand. Property was no matter in times like these.

The landscape came alive as the pack broke from the mist and charged towards Heatherbloom's heart. Horns! Conor thought as he drew his sword. He had never seen a pack so large. There must have been two-dozen wolves or more charging across the hummocks and braes.

Rory and two others were suddenly there with bows and arrows. They drew aim on the approaching animals. Bowstrings twanged and two of the archers found marks. But the loss of a mere two among four and twenty was not enough to frighten or slow down the pack. Snarling savagely, they continued up the slope. Conor's small hairs rose. There was some magic about, and it was not one he liked the feel of for it possessed an almost bitter burn.

Angus suddenly returned with a sword and targe. Some of his men were equally armed, but the majority had little more than rakes, hoes, and rocks.

More arrows flew, and this time three wolves yelped in pain and dropped like stones. The rest just ran over the top of the fallen as though driven by some force they could not resist. And after that, no more arrows could be drawn for the pack had reached the village and were going at the men as though they were sheep. Conor braced himself as a wolf lunged for his throat. His sword cut fur and flesh with practiced ease. The body of the wolf flung off to one side. Another came, and Conor dispatched it with a single thrust of his long sword through its chest. As it fell at his feet, he reached back and pulled out his long dirk, wanting two weapons in hand.

He heard a man screaming in pain. Women and children shrieked in terror as they crouched in the cottages. Some of the wolves went to the cottages and attacked the closed doors. Conor could do no more than concentrate on keeping the wolves at bay. *This is not natural,* he thought. Wolves rarely attacked men unless starved or rabid with the foaming madness. These wolves were clearly neither.

This butchery is war, he told himself as he was forced to kill yet another beast.

He turned in time to see Angus fending off one beast with sword and targe, but just as he laid the wolf down with the targe and stabbed it with his sword, another crept up on his back and started to lunge. Conor shouted and dove at the beast. It turned, snarled, and started to rush Conor instead.

Fate chose that moment to play a nasty hand. Conor stepped in blood too slick to allow him to stay balanced at such a rapid pace. He jerked and felt a muscle spasm as he fought to stay on his feet. He threw out his arms and the wolf lunged for that opening. Snapping jaws clamped down on his left arm. Gauntlets and bracers kept Conor from losing life's blood and having those fangs rend flesh. But the wolf's momentum was powerful enough to rock Conor back. Jaws clamped about his wrist. The wolf shook his arm as though to snap the neck of a hare. Pain shot through his wrist and nerves screamed as he lost his grip on the long dirk. The weight of the wolf bore Conor down, and it showed no sign of releasing him. He hit the ground solidly, nearly knocking all the breath out of his lungs and barely keeping his grip on his sword.

With no other weapon available to thrust from such a close range, Conor could do no more than whack the wolf in the head with the heavy pommel. It took more than one pounding blow to convince the wolf to let go. Shrieking in pain, it opened its jaws and fell back. Conor pushed himself to his knees just as it tried to lunge at him again. His blade snapped around in an arch and severed the animal's head.

Conor had just climbed to his feet when he saw a sight that froze his heart. At least fifty wolves now formed a semi-circle around the heart of the village. *Howt awa, what are these beasts that they fear neither fire nor men?* They stood larger than any wolves he had seen in his life. Indeed, they reminded Conor of the ancient beasts he had heard tales of when he was young, but the last of those large wolves were thought to have died out ages ago.

Now they stood shoulder to shoulder as soldiers mustering to face an enemy. And yet some of them whimpered and lowered their heads as though restless with fear. The men of Heatherbloom who were still on their feet were forming a line to defend themselves. Conor was pleased to see that Angus was still among them, though he was bleeding from several bites. They eyed the wolves as warily as the wolves eyed them.

Why do they not attack? Conor thought.

Some of the wolves started tucking tails and lowering their heads. It was then that the familiar brush of a breeze across the small hairs of his neck alerted Conor. Daring not to take his eyes off the semicircle, he could not help but wonder what it was that held them at bay.

At least until he heard his adopted son's voice ring like a herald in a court.

"Go back!" Rhoyd shouted. "I set you free! Go back!"

Set you free? Conor thought. *What in the name of Cernunnos does he mean by that?* The lad was daft if he thought mere beasts would obey him.

The wolves seemed reluctant to obey. Then to Conor's surprise, some of them whined and turned their tails and began to slink down the slope back into the mist, but others held their place. And one or two began to advance. Embolden, others that remained followed, and somewhere out in the mist, Conor felt that miasma growing stronger.

"Close your eyes!" Rhoyd shouted.

Conor obeyed. There was an explosion as the fires all around the village rose hot on his skin. Behind his eyelids, it looked as though the sun was rising on his face. He heard the frightened shouts of men and lupine yelps of terror, and the sound of a mounted army suddenly riding away.

Then silence, save the wailing of the women and the moans of the men.

Conor opened his eyes. He blinked in the gloaming where the shadows had grown long and thick. At the top of the rise, he could make out the cottage of Angus' late mother. Before it, two figures were visible.

Eithne's face was stiff with worry. In front of her stood Rhoyd. The lad trembled as he held a flicker of white fire in the palms of his hands.

Of the wolves, there was no sign.

Rhoyd was dreaming again, but this time there was no chase across the moors. There was no beast with a shape distorted and uncertain. Instead, he was standing on a parapet while thunder and lightning played across the sky. He was certain that it was daytime, but there was darkness everywhere, an unnatural sky where the sun fought a useless battle against the thickness of clouds, and the world seemed bathed in a strange bluish light.

Below there was a courtyard, and as Rhoyd watched a woman with the head of a wolf brandished a sword. Beside her stood a man whose short stature was set off by a stocky, muscular build. He had a long mane of dark hair that crawled down his bare back so that it looked more like a pelt. Stripped to his waist, he carried a spear with a rowan haft. The steel point glowed with faint white luminescence.

There is magic in that steel, Rhoyd thought as he stared at the sight.

Littering the cobbles of the courtyard before this man were the bodies of both black and white hounds. The white ones' ears were tipped in red, and Rhoyd had some faint recollection of a story Conor told him about Seelie hounds. The black ones had red eyes and bloody fangs. There had been a savage battle here, and the hounds had killed one another from the looks of it.

Beyond the canine carnage, between two tall stones and wrapped in shadows was a thing that had the appearance of a man. But it was tall and wore black armor, and its face was white like the belly of a fish, and its features carried a hint of dragon and demon. A Shadow Lord...

Beside it crouched the beast that had stalked Rhoyd in his nightmares. Even now, the monster sniffed the air as though sensing Rhoyd, and he wondered if this was where it had been chasing him from all these nights. He stood still as the stones of the wall to his back and watched. He gave up trying to duck behind the rail and hide. His limbs would not obey him.

"Is that the best you have?" the Shadow Lord asked. "You would slay me with mere hounds?"

The short man stepped forward and raised his spear. His eyes were amber like those of the Shadow Lord.

"Nay, *Dubh Sealgair*," he said. "I have a greater gift for you. I call it *Eigh Loisg* and it was forged in *Fuar Teailach* by the *An Gobha Mor* and tempered in the belly of the Lord of Water that it might carry the power to send you back to Annwn with the rest of your wretched kin."

"You cannot slay me. Or did your Fearfaolan bitch of a mother not tell you who I am?"

"Yes, Father, I know who you are, and I know that I am your son," he said, and the Shadow Lord flinched. "But my mother has raised me to be your doom, and I shall avenge her and the people you have condemned in the name of the Dark Mother."

With an angry shout, he raised the spear. Great bolts of lightning jagged out of the sky and struck the points of the stones. A dark portal began to open. Another bolt flashed, and the crackling fingers rebound and rushed straight at the Shadow Lord. They struck the Shadow Lord in the chest, driving him back against the mouth of the dark portal. Just as he fell into its grasp, the beast howled and lunged at his son. Jaws snapped within inches of the man's throat. Great paws thumped his chest, shoving him to the ground.

Rhoyd gasped for he felt those paws strike him and smelled the hot fetid breath of doom on his own face. Before he could fathom why, he heard the screams that snapped him out of sleep. He opened his eyes.

Eithne was scrambling to her feet. Rhoyd struggled to get on his own and wipe away the last of his dream. He could hear men shouting and the snarls of wolves.

Wolves!

"Blessed Brother," Eithne cried. She had gone to the windows to look out when jaws snapped at the opening, forcing her backwards. A wolf was trying to scramble into the window.

"Gath siud buail!" Rhoyd shouted.

His mage bolt smacked the beast in the muzzle. With a startled yelp, the wolf jerked back. Eithne rushed back to the window. She slammed the rickety little wooden shutters closed and jammed the makeshift bolt back in place.

"Blessed Brother, what is happening?" she cried.

The horses stamped and squealed restlessly, their hooves thundering on the ground. And from the yelp of the wolves, Rhoyd knew that Battlebrute was on the attack.

But where was Conor?

Rhoyd stretched mage senses, searching the mass of living auras that filled the air until he felt the familiar bronze warmth. It was hot with the fury of battle, and Rhoyd felt the death of the wolves that dared to attack his adopted father. He could also feel the darkness that was swelling out in the edges of the world, a strange power from ancient times, bitter with the essence of a demon. Its essence was flooding into the wolves as well, and Rhoyd could feel it commanding the beasts to attack and kill.

This must stop! he thought, for death was screaming on the currents of the air, feeding the essence of the beast and making it stronger. *That malevolence must be vanquished before everyone dies. They do not do this willingly!*

"I have to stop them," Rhoyd said as he drew back his mage senses and opened his eyes. He scrambled for the door.

"Rhoyd, no!" Eithne cried and rushed to stop him. "The wolves..."

She seized him by one arm as he reached the door. But he was determined to get out. With a shout, he shook off her grasp, jerking the door open and flying out into the gloaming. Eithne charged after him. For a fleeting moment, dizziness assailed him. He staggered to a stop on the slope.

There were wolves everywhere and they were massing for the attack. Rhoyd jerked essence from the world, collecting the power into his hands. He whispered *"Loisg,"* and white fire flared to life. As one, the wolves stopped and drew together, looking up the hill at him. They suddenly rushed together, forming a semi-circle, standing shoulder to shoulder.

They will not leave, something whispered in the wind. He could see it in the looks in their eyes. Whatever had a grasp on them was struggling to maintain its hold. Fear, anger, rage, all assailed him from afar. He coaxed the flames stronger and felt the power retreating slightly.

It cannot bear my light...

The power was fighting him. Some of the wolves began to whine like whipped curs and lowered their heads.

I will make them leave, Rhoyd retorted. He didn't want to kill them if he did not have to.

"Why don't they attack?" he heard one of the men asking. He scanned their numbers and saw Conor getting off his knees, meeting the wolves eye to eye.

He's hurt, Rhoyd thought.

He filled his lungs and shouted, "Go back! I set you free! Go back!"

Some of the wolves fled straight away. Others

hesitated, heads lowered, and still others held their place. Large beasts they were, dark of pelt and nearly as tall as shaggy moor ponies, and they began to stalk the men at the fire, refusing to leave.

There's nothing else I can do...

He took a deep breath and shouted, "Close your eyes!"

Some of the men might have obeyed as Rhoyd concentrated on the fires. He pulled their essence to him and hissed *"Loisg mhor!"* he fed his power into the flames. The power he had gathered practically flew from his hands and entered the flames in the pit. The thunder of power tumbled on his ears as the flames roared. There was an explosion, and white fire spread high and wide, and for a moment, Rhoyd feared that he had overdone it, that he would burn the men as he frightened the wolves. It looked as though the sun had come to visit the world.

No animal had the courage to remain. Even the essence of malaise that had controlled the wolves was unable to keep that control intact. With screams and yelps, the wolves cowed and turned and fled, like a cavalry retreating into the wilds. Then silence laid claim to the world.

Conor charged up the hillside, holding his left arm close as though it pained him. His presence broke Eithne out of her trance. Conor looked down at Rhoyd and winked, then looked at Eithne.

"Are you two all right?" he asked.

"We're fine, but you're hurt," she said.

"I'll be fine until you've seen to the others, woman," Conor said.

"But Rhoyd?"

"I'll stay with the lad," Conor said.

Rhoyd sighed with relief.

At least he wasn't in trouble.

This is so strange, Eithne thought as she crossed the village to tend to the need of the men. Behind her, she sensed Conor had need as well. Oh, he might think he could hide it from her, but she felt it all the same. *One would think after all these years of marriage he would remember that,* she thought.

She would never understand why men thought they had to lie about pain.

With one exception, the villagers were not badly hurt. A few suffered bites. The one sufferer was an older man whose rake had done little to protect him from the savagery of one of the wolves, and he had taken several bites to the arms and shoulders. She tended him first, assisted by the same women who had lent her a hand during Sioban's birthing. They seemed more subdued about this man's wounds than they had about the birth. Eithne showed them how to set the splints on the breaks, and how to stitch the wounds, then left them to finish while she moved on to the next man. The rest, she attended swiftly, using Diancecht's gift to heal any who had a need.

Laird MacLean came to see how she was doing just as she was completing the last bandage on the smith MacDermot's cuts--he had slipped in the muck and done more damage to his knees on the rocks--and she noticed at once that the laird was limping.

"You were bitten?" she asked, pointing to his leg.

"'Tis but a scratch," the laird assured her.

"Let me be the judge of that," she said. "Here, sit down."

Angus looked like he might not take her orders well. But then he seated himself on the bench that Dermot was deserting and extended his leg for her examination. A cut ran the length of his shin. Not deep enough to require stitching, but it needed cleaning all the same.

"Yer lad was a brave one, coming out and calling the fire as he did," Angus said.

Eithne tried not to frown. "Well, I do hope your clan will not hold that against him. He's only a lad, after all."

Angus nodded. "'Tis not like it was in the old days," he

63

said almost wistfully, she noticed. "Folks what could make the wind blow and bend the trees and call the stones and the fire and the water to their hands were thought to be wonders of the Old Ones. But the dark times fell on us after that damnable Hound tried to take our kingdoms."

Eithne sighed. "Yes, the Last War left many distrustful."

"It made fools of some," Angus said. "My mother was a good woman. Before the war, there were many who came here seeking her counsel. After the war, they wouldna give her the courtesy 'o a simple 'good morrow, Mistress,' let alone ask for her help. That cottage up there where you stay, we built it, my sons and I, because it was making the rest of the villagers uneasy to have her living in our midst."

"Do you think I should warn Conor to keep a closer eye on Rhoyd?" she asked.

Angus shook his head and smiled. "There's the rub, Mistress MacManahan. They saw what your lad did to save them, and now they think him a blessing. But I imagine it is good that you and your man are leaving tomorrow, as in a few days, they are as apt to curse him for bringing the beasts on us."

She arched her eyebrows and gently spread a paste of comfrey on his leg. "Then it is good we are leaving," she said. "And I thank you for your hospitality."

"You are most welcome," he said.

Eithne finished her task, laying a strip of linen across the wound and binding it in place. Then gathering her gear, she headed back up the hill.

Conor's need still spoke to her as she stepped into the cottage. He was sitting in the chair, Rhoyd beside him looking concerned. Conor's face was pale.

"Have you had enough pain for one day?" Eithne asked.

Conor shot her a dark look that faded into resignation.

64

"Aye, it hurts, woman," he said. He offered her his wrist. She frowned, taking in the sight of bruises where he had removed his gauntlet and bracers. There were no cuts, but clearly the wrist had been stressed.

"A sprain," she said, gently running fingers over the surface and watching him flinch. "Easily dealt with, but it will be stiff for a day or two. Good thing it's not your sword hand. May haps, I should give you a draught so you can sleep tonight?"

Conor looked as though he might object. But he sighed and nodded. *You need sleep as much as I do,* she thought, though she would never have said so aloud, certainly not with Rhoyd so close at hand. As it was, the lad was looking worn and tired.

She smiled for him, then laid her hands on Conor's wrist and closed her eyes.

"Blessed Brother, hear my plea..." she said softly, letting the prayer flow from her lips. The power of Diancecht came to her as it had been doing all day, and she fed it into Conor's arm. She opened her eyes and saw him leaning back, eyes closed, the knot of tension between his brows lessening. With a sigh, she stopped and let go. Conor smiled. Rhoyd giggled and rubbed his nose.

"That tickled," Rhoyd said and grinned.

FIVE

He told himself it was the wind. The exhaustion of sleep kept Rhoyd from dreaming, but he woke up put of the dark depths of sleep to an eerie song.

A wolf? He could not be certain. It might have been one of the strays he had scattered still wandering about the moors. Rhoyd sat up on his pallet and carefully cast about with mage senses, not wanting to alert Conor. But Conor had fought hard and was battle weary. The heaviness of his snores told Rhoyd that Conor was deep asleep. The normally soft burr was a rough rumble, like thunder in the distance when a storm was brewing.

Rhoyd sighed, for he had to admit that even that heavy sound was a comfort. It meant Conor was at hand and Rhoyd was safe.

Or am I?

In truth, the miasma that had filtered in and out when the wolves attacked--the miasma that awakened Rhoyd before--was still flitting about the moors far away. He could feel its essence, a faint bitterness on his tongue.

Demon.

But why would there be a demon out here.

Frowning, he pressed harder, mindful that such activity could get him into trouble.

The demon was circling outside the furthest edge of the glen. Closer in Rhoyd sensed that something else stirred. Something possessed of a vague hint of familiarity.

She's out there.

Rhoyd pushed his blankets aside. He glanced at the

hearth where he had seen Brina huddling, stirring ashes all last night. She was not there, but he sensed she was somewhere outside.

Carefully pulling on his boots, Rhoyd crept over to the door. Conor still snored. Eithne stirred lightly then settled again.

Rhoyd lifted the small bar that held the door shut and praying that the hinges did not squeal, he opened the door and stepped out into the night.

The song was louder, though it was not a song that Conor would sing before the hearth fire. Instead, it was an eerie keen, a wild voice wailing like some bogie from one of Conor's tales. As Rhoyd recalled, there was the tale of the washerwoman who cried as she washed the bloody clothes of those meant to die.

Was he hearing the harbinger of someone's death?

My own?

He shivered and considered turning back. Why should he go out and risk his life at night? But the soft keen broke his thoughts with sadness. He let mage eyes rove the amber circles of torch and firelight and tried to peer into the shadows beyond their glow.

Brina stood just at the edge of the outermost circle of light. He could see the hints of heather and stones bathed in darkness through her translucent form. The wind tossed her long white hair and her marriage plaidie as it played with his own. How? He had seen spirits waffling in the wind like weeds when there was not wind for him to feel, but there was a stiff cold breeze, unnatural even for this time of the year, and it was pushing against him.

His thoughts were interrupted when Brina beckoned him with long fingers. Rhoyd hesitated. The last time he gave in to her summons, she had shown him her death. He was not eager to repeat that.

Brina seemed to sense his unease. She offered a smile, and her voice reached inside his head. Fear not. It is safe. There is someone you must meet before you go on to your destiny...

She gestured again and began to walk up the hill. Rhoyd cast about with mage senses but felt nothing close. Indeed, as he stretched those senses, the malaise retreated as though not wishing to be discovered nearby.

Rhoyd took a deep breath and started up the hill. Brina walked in among the ancient boulders littering the landscape. Instead of following the trail they had taken to look for the thief, she was heading another way and now his curiosity got the better of him.

The path she chose was steeper too, and it required grasping clumps of heather and jagged stones to keep from slipping back. Steeper still it grew. Rhoyd stopped and put a hand to a stone when the climbing began to test his lungs. And withdrew with a gasp when he felt some faint essence of life within. He stared at the stone. Time had weathered it, but there were the barest hints of features. Rhoyd peered at them, trying to make them out when suddenly Brina's face appeared as she pushed herself through the stone. He strangled a shout, stumbling back, managing to snag a snarled little tree to keep from tumbling down the steep path.

"What did you do that for?" he hissed.

"Let the Stone Folks sleep," she said.

"Stone Folk?" Rhoyd had heard tales of them from Conor who said they were short men of the ancient world, well versed in masonry, mining and iron. Some had been smiths in the days before the Great Cataclysm. "This was one of the Stone Folk?"

"When the world was new, there were Stone Folk in many lands," Brina said. "They didn't all crawl out of Ymir's nose. Now come, we waste precious time. The one you must meet will not wait long for fear of the beast."

Rhoyd looked around at the scattering of boulders. "Were all of these Stone Folk?" he asked as he followed her floating form.

Brina shook her head. "Some are just stones."

"Were they good Stone Folk or bad?"

"Save your breath for climbing, boy," she scolded and flitted further ahead.

With a snort of indignation, Rhoyd pushed his hair from his eyes and continued to climb. They passed the point where he had tripped and hit his head, continuing to move upward. Just when he thought his lungs would explode, Brina stopped. She had reached the summit--or at least a large ledge, the back of which opened into a cave.

Rhoyd froze. Animal odors wafted from that cave, the musky scent of canines, the scent of meat being roasted, the stench of unwashed skin. He covered his nose.

"Do not show such disrespect," Brina scolded, coming close enough that he felt the chill of her essence.

He hesitated and dropped his hand. Wincing at the rank odors, he tried to shallow his breathing.

"Stand here and wait," Brina said, and she floated into the cave, disappearing from even mage sight.

Moments passed. Rhoyd heard the trill of a moor owl on the hunt and the rustle of its wings as it passed overhead. He stretched mage senses to follow its path of flight and felt death when the bird found prey swiftly. Beyond that, he sensed the lingering dark, keeping its distance. Then his attention was drawn back to the cave when a shadow stirred from the mouth.

His heart flew into his throat as a pair of large wolves emerged. Their yellow eyes fixed him with a predator's stare. Rhoyd stumbled back, looking for the quickest means of getting down the path. Then he glanced at the wolves again, wondering why they did not charge.

A woman's figure wrapped in a woolen cloak greeted him. Her face was hidden inside the hood. Long strands of her hair leaked out from those shadows. The strands were grey in the moonlight. She put a hand on the ruff of each wolf, and in turn they sat down like a pair of sentries. Brina drifted into his line of view as well.

"Rhoyd," Brina said softly. He flinched to hear his

name spoken, confused at first to think that she would know it. But then he reminded himself that she was a spirit who lingered in her cottage and probably heard Conor and Eithne speak it. "Let me introduce you to Greymoon, Mother of the Pack of Heatherbloom, the last descendants of the Faolanwold to live upon these moors."

Rhoyd held his place, uncertain now just what to do. Greymoon pushed back her hood to reveal a face. A wolf's face, but the eyes had human irises, and they were blue like his own.

"So, this is the one who discovered little Henslayer in the cave?" Greymoon asked.

Rhoyd blinked as memories flooded him. "She hit me with a chicken," he said.

Greymoon's canines showed when she smiled. "She was frightened," she said. "She knew you could see her in the dark as we do."

Rhoyd took a deep breath. "Are you the Fearfaolan?" he asked.

"That is our ancient name," Greymoon said. "You have seen us in your dreams, have you not? Just as you have seen him."

"You know about my dreams?" Rhoyd asked.

"I have sensed them," she said. "The scent of your distress has come to me and mine on the wind. We know that you have seen the Dark One."

"The demon?" Rhoyd glanced out in the dark and shivered. "It's out there now," he said.

"Yes, and it knows that you will soon reach the place where it once lived with its master, and that when you do, there is a chance the darkness will seek you out and try to use you to set the Shadow Lord free. For you are the one who carries the brightest flame of ancient times within, and when the time of the Darkening comes, you will be the light of the world."

"What can I do to stop it?"

"Can you stop the wind?" Greymoon asked.

Rhoyd frowned. "Yes," he said.

71

She quirked her eyes in the manner of one arching their brows. "Then you will know what to do," she said. "It is what you are born to do."

Rhoyd was not so certain that he liked that idea. Even now, as often as his Uncle Fenelon had badgered him to learn more intricate spells that his Aunt Genna was unwilling to teach, he hated feeling like he was being prepared for a task he never wanted.

"Is this why you brought me here, Brina?" he asked. "To be told what I already know?"

"Greymoon is a warrior and Lore Mother to her pack," Brina said. "I merely thought she would be able to tell you what you needed to know before you journeyed on to Faolanwold."

"I just want to stop the dreams," Rhoyd said.

Greymoon stepped out from between her guardians and drew closer. He smelled the musky odor of her pelt. The hands she slipped out of the warmth of her cloak were as human as his, except for the fine layer of down that was visible at the edges of her sleeves. She held out her hand to him and reluctantly, he took it.

"The dreams will stop when you decide to put darkness back into its cage," she said.

"The darkness?"

"The demon you sense out there must be imprisoned in stone again."

"In stone?" Rhoyd said. "But it wasn't me that let him out." He turned a scowl on Brina. "You set it free."

Brina lowered her head and nodded. "It is true, my folly set him free, but my death stopped me from undoing my mistake and setting it right. My blood released the beast, and only one of the blood can put him back."

"Why me?" Rhoyd asked.

Brina reached out and touched his heart. He was tempted to draw away, remembering his last encounter with her, but there was no sudden rush of visions this time. She sighed.

"As Greymoon said, you are the light," she said. "You are the one who will bring back the balance when order and chaos go to war. You will unite the Darkness with the Light. It is your purpose, child, whether you like it or not."

"Well, I don't like it," Rhoyd said and pulled away from her and Greymoon, seeking a safe path down the steep side of the hill he had climbed. He could see the bare twinkle of the village watch fires far below and longed to be there.

Greymoon was suddenly in his path.

"I will seek you out when you reach the far side of Coldforge," she said. "I will tell you the lore so that you will know. And I will give you my word that the Fearfaolan and our wild brethren will be watching your back. We are sworn to keep the Balance of All Things just as you are. We will not let them do you harm if we can help it."

"I am supposed to trust wolves that attacked my family?"

"They were not our wolves. Those wild ones were possessed by shadow wolves conjured by the demon so they could attack in the gloaming. Did you not wonder why your white fire caused them to flee? You destroyed the shadow wolves and set the wild ones free."

Rhoyd closed his eyes. "I want to go back now," he said. "I want to go back to my family."

"They shall attend you," she said and pointed to the pair of wolves who rose to stand. "They will show you a safer path and see to it that you reach the village unharmed. You have no reason to fear harm from them. Come. Let us have your scent that we might know you."

"My scent?"

She took his hand again, gently coaxing him towards the cave. The odor of the wolves bit into his nostrils. He fought the urge to wrinkle his nose again.

Greymoon drew him into the mouth of the cave. There was a tunnel descending into the rock, and it twisted back on itself. The last of the moonlight was gone. Shadows filled his eyes at first, but then, his eyes adjusted to the cavern's depth. Or was that a light ahead. The tunnel turned once more. Greymoon stopped suddenly and Rhoyd realized he was in a large cavern, much like a hall. Small fires were set about and around them, a multitude of creatures like her, men and women and children with wolf heads and human bodies, and none of them standing taller than him.

There must have been three-dozen or more. They all watched him with human eyes. And scattered among them, he saw real wolves.

"Come my pack kin, my children. Come my Wild Brethren," Greymoon said. "This is Rhoyd, the Ard Magister. Know him. Know that he has my word that we will protect him and see no harm comes to him, for he will be the Balance of All Things."

Bodies came towards him in mass. Wolves whined as they walked up to him, heads bowed, tails wagging hesitantly. He realized then that Greymoon spoke true. They were not the same wolves he had freed from the demon's control, for they were larger and cleaner. They sniffed him and then moved away, allowing others to come to him. The Fearfaolan as well approached him in the manner of dogs seeking a master's approval. *But I am not their master,* he thought. They did not seem to care. Just as the wolves had sniffed him, the Fearfaolan sniffed him as well. Some of them had cold noses, and he tried not to flinch as they brushed against his hands.

Finally, the last one had touched him. They drew back in a circle, and then as one, they raised their heads, Fearfaolan and wolves alike, and filled the cavern with an eerie song.

The same song that brought him out of his sleep. They sang it, harmonizing wolf cries into a rich chorus. The sound was almost deafening.

It stopped abruptly when Greymoon raised her hands. She turned to the two wolves that stood back when they had entered the caverns. "They will take you back now.

Go with our blessing. I will see you on the other side of Coldforge."

Rhoyd was not sure if he should bow or just leave. The two large wolves were suddenly on either side of him, drawing him out of the pack, herding him out of the cave. One of them crouched before him and made strange moaning sounds as it looked at him. Rhoyd hesitated. *What now?* he thought.

Greymoon was suddenly there, smiling. "Brown Chaser says your legs are too short to keep up with him and his mate Wind Sidhe. He will carry you back."

Rhoyd reluctantly straddled the wolf. It was nearly as large as a pony and when it rose to all fours, he had to grab handfuls of the ruff at its shoulders to stay on its back. At once, Brown Chaser started off at a swift pace. Rhoyd gasped in amazement and grasped with his knees. The wolf moved swiftly across heather and stone, charging this way and that. The mad rush quite took Rhoyd's breath away. *I'm riding a wolf! A real wolf! Who will believe this?*

They made the descent more rapidly than he could ever have done on his own. His fear went flying with the wind as the excitement of the race rushed into him. It was almost like being a hawk, swooping low over the rough ground until at last they reached the edge of the village.

Only then did Brown Chaser and his mate stop. Rhoyd hurriedly dropped from the wolf's back, giving Brown Chaser a pat on the shoulder.

"Thank you, that was..."

Before he could finish, the wolves looked up in fright, then turned and fled for the hills.

Rhoyd glanced back to see what had sent them fleeing.

Conor stood at the corner of the cottage, his mouth agape.

I think I'm in trouble now.

Rhoyd sighed and looked up at his adopted father.

"I'm sorry," he said. "I can explain."

"Did I just see you riding a wolf?" Conor asked, his

speech slurred.

Rhoyd bit his lip. It occurred to him that Conor was probably still dizzy from Eithne's pain draught.

"Yes," he said carefully.

"Good," Conor said. "Because if I didn't, I'd say I was dreaming. Come on. Let's get back inside. Ye can tell me all about it in the morning. I'll know by then whether or not I should give ye a hiding for scaring me that way."

"You don't know now?" Rhoyd ventured.

Conor looked down from his great height. His eyes were bleary as he leaned over Rhoyd, forcing him to take a step back.

"Be mindful what you say, lad," Conor growled. "The woman's weeds are messing with my aim or I'd clout ye for that bit of lip. My head will be much clearer in the morning." He suddenly took hold of Rhoyd by the nape and gave him a shake of admonishment before adding, "Assuming I remember any of this. Now inside with ye, and no more of this blether."

Rhoyd bit his tongue rather than say that the only one blethering was Conor. The grasp on his neck loosened, and he was pushed towards the cottage, but not before Conor's free hand came around and mussed Rhoyd's hair in a fond gesture.

"Wild rogue," Conor muttered. "Riding wolves as big as moor ponies. What next? Bears?

Rhoyd allowed himself a secret smile of relief and quickened his pace to enter the cottage with Conor close behind.

SIX

They rode for most of the day, leaving Heatherbloom far behind as they followed the road that meandered the moors. Conor kept a watchful eye out for wolves. And though he felt something was out there watching his family ride past, he never saw the cause of his unease.

Just as well. What happened back in Heatherbloom last night still haunted his thoughts, and he would glance at Rhoyd from time to time to see if the lad was sensing anything Conor could not. Rhoyd seemed distracted, enough so to put Conor on edge. *And after that stunt ye pulled last night...What were ye thinking, lad, going out in the moonlight to ride wild wolves like some gormless fey thing.*

Conor didn't want to think what could have happened had he not been roused to relieve himself. Had he not found Rhoyd sitting atop that wolf like a cavalryman returning from the battlefields. He was still not entirely sure that it had not been a dream.

Rhoyd had seemed so unconcerned. He said he had gone for a walk to relieve his nature and gotten lost. That the wolves had come to his rescue and brought him back safely.

Rescued by wolves? Were they the same ones that attacked us earlier? The ones you set free? Conor was not willing to let the conversation go. The lad was being too vague to make Conor happy.

Rhoyd simply shrugged and said, "I don't think they were the same wolves. They seemed...different. Magical. Maybe they were like the seelie wolves you're always telling me stories about."

"That makes no sense, lad," Conor had said in a tone that caused Rhoyd to hitch back in uncertainty. "Wolves don't rescue lost lads. They usually eat them."

There had been a brief moment when Rhoyd looked scared, and Conor felt his own gut twist with guilt. "Look, I am not angry," Conor said in a gentler tone, "but it just doesn't make sense to me that you go wandering in the dark and come back riding wolves." Rhoyd merely shrugged once more. The furtive wandering of those blue eyes said there was more to this tale than the lad had revealed. *Is he lying to me? Why?*

What was this power that convinced his son to wander the moors on a bogie night?

Conor was grateful for the daylight, for though clouds tempered the sunlight into a dull haze, and patches of mist roamed the lower reaches of the moors, he could not completely shake his distrust of what was transpiring in the life of his little family. Soon enough, signs of civilization began to appear and put him at ease. Cow pats by the road, wagon ruts freshly made. And the scent of cooking fires and cattle and sheep. Yes, they must be close to some place. They would sleep in more civilized quarters, assuming Rhoyd's dreams did not cause them to be driven out. By the horns of Cernunnos, please let him sleep this night. No more wandering in the dark. Conor had to admit it was the first good sleep he'd had.

It occurred to him to wonder why Rhoyd had not dreamed. Or if he had, why he had not awoken in a state of terror. Conor would have to remember to ask the lad later.

If I remember.

The road took a turn, clambering up and over a hill, and from the top it afforded a wonderful sight for Conor's weary eyes. Yes, there was civilization here. An orderly arrangement of farms and crops grew on the uneven ground surrounding the next rise. A hill fort at one time, it now carried two walls, an off-center keep and signs of an old double moat. But all was now filled with closely set cottages behind a stone and wooden palisade.

Oddly, there were no marker stones close by to tell Conor where he was, but he had been this way before. Or near it on another road some years ago. This had to be Coldforge. And even if it wasn't, the presence of a town was enough to make him smile. It was not that he could not live easily on his native highlands with little more than his plaidie to shelter him, but he knew that his travels with Eithne had made warm beds in comfortable inns a welcome venture more and more as the years passed.

Am I getting too old for this work? Mercenary, husband, father. *Why in the name of Cernunnos do I suddenly feel so old?* He was only seven and thirty. Far from old.

He glanced at Rhoyd again. The lad was poking into one of his saddlebags, putting away the book he had used to occupy himself the last league or so. Now he looked up and stared at the small township.

"Is that where we're going to stay tonight?" he ventured.

"We hope," Conor said and put heels to Battlebrute once more, quickening the pace to an easy trot down the moor road.

It took little time to reach the outer gates. Conor stopped and glanced around. No one blocked the opening, but he suspected the murder holes were being watched and the portcullis was down. Locals threaded in and out of the small postern gate that sat open even as he drew rein and indicated for Eithne and Rhoyd to hold back.

Looking up, he spied a guard leaning over the edge of the gatehouse atop a stone and wooden palisade, looking back down at him.

"Are ye lost?" the guard asked.

Conor shook his head. "No more than most," he replied, and the guard grinned in a good-natured manner. "Is this Coldforge?"

"Aye, it is," the guard replied. "What be yer business

here, stranger?"

"I'm Conor MacManahan," Conor said. "This is my wife who is a True Healer, and this is our son. We have come from Heatherbloom where Laird Angus MacLean said I should ask for the smith MacFee whom the laird called cousin and said would give us shelter for the night."

The guard's smile widened. "Shelter with Mad MacFee. Ye be a brave man."

Conor frowned. Mad MacFee? Angus had said nothing about his cousin being mad.

"Come on in, then," the guard said. "If our good cousin in Heatherbloom sent ye, then yer most welcome, though why he told ye to shelter with Mad MacFee is beyond my understanding."

"Then yer kin to the smith?" Conor ventured.

"Aye, our fathers were brothers. Fergus MacFee at yer service."

He gestured to someone inside the wall. The flow of folk going through the small door ceased and a couple of guards stepped out and urged everyone to step back from the gatehouse. Conor eased Battlebrute away as he heard the crank of a windlass and watched as the gate opened. The jagged bottom that came out of the trench looked like a monstrous overbite.

"Tell me, Fergus MacFee," Conor called. "Why do they call your cousin mad?"

Several locals chuckled as though this was an old joke. Fergus merely shrugged. "I dinna ken. I suppose 'tis because he looks mad all the time. Ye'll find him just off the market. Take the straight path through the inner wall then follow the wide road up the hill to the market. Then turn left and just follow the din. Ye'll find him easily enough with yer ears."

"My thanks to ye, Fergus MacFee," Conor said, though now he was not certain he should be thankful. He put heels to Battlebrute and aimed him at the maw of the gate. The warhorse's hooves clattered on the wooden bridge crossing the outer moat, and Maudie and Moonface quickly added to the din, slipping in with the stream of local folk determined to get about their own business.

Once inside the first gate, Conor saw that the second moat ringing the older section of the hill fort had long ago been filled with a jumble of cottages with their backs pressed to the inner wall. Small patches of gardens grew among the houses, and livestock were penned in some of the remaining gaps. It amazed him that folks could live crammed so close together.

The second gate was reached by an earthen bridge of stone and logs, and it was little more than a break in what must have once been a stronghold's wall. At one time, there might have been more stones to it. He could see places where crumbled towers once stood like sentinels. When the village sprawled and grew inside an older fortification, many of the stones and rocks were carted away to build other things, like the lone tower that rose to one side of the entrance and had its own wall and gate.

They rode on through and found the wide path. Strewn with cobbles, Conor was willing to bet it became a wash out of mud in the rainy season. Nor did it go straight, but lazily circled and climbed the height of the hill, passing between rows of daub and wattle cottages until it reached the top.

As they ambled into the center of the village proper, there was much activity. Market day was in full swing, though now it was winding down. Merchants were hawking a variety of wares. A few heads turned towards Conor and his family, but he saw little more than mild curiosity and friendly smiles. *Coldforge must get a fair wheen 'o strangers passing through,* Conor thought. No one looked tense or worried. Some folks even held up their wares and shouted for his attention. He merely waved them off.

Around the market houses were jammed shoulder to shoulder and growing upward. Smaller paths, most of them wide enough for two riding abreast cut off at several angles. To his left, even above the babble of local merchants, Conor could hear the faithful din of hammer and anvil.

Odd, Conor thought as he glanced around. Though there were folk aplenty in the market, the very highest point of the hill fort stood deserted. Occupying that space stood an old stone smithy. Why was it empty? The locals enjoying their market day gave it a wide berth. A few made warding signs, touching forehead, lips, and heart. Others shaded their eyes from the structure by placing a hand to the side of their face.

Cold prickled Conor's skin. He glanced at Rhoyd who stared at the structure in fascination. Conor frowned.

"This way," he said and urged Rhoyd and Eithne to follow, making certain that Rhoyd obeyed. The lad almost reluctantly turned his horse from the sight and wandered after Conor. Indeed, Rhoyd looked longingly back at the structure.

Time to nip that in the bud, Conor thought. He threw back his head and started to sing.

"Oh, I hear the hammer ringing,
The anvil singing from within,
The smith is in his smithy,
And he's making such a din,
He'll wake the men from Bonny Bough
Up to the Ferlie Glen..."

The song did its work. Rhoyd looked forward and giggled. Eithne rolled her eyes.

"That's all we need," she said. "Conor offending our host with that song."

"It's not a bad song, woman. I learned it from a smith, remember?"

She said nothing, which was fine by Conor. The prickling sensation receded as they followed the sounds away from the center. The path Conor took turned right, and then left where it opened into a broad yard where wagon wheels and metal scrap lie in heaps off to one side. With them was a large handcart heaped with large brownish clumps.

"Since when does a smith need a wagon load of dirt?" Conor muttered.

"That's not dirt," Rhoyd said as he rode up beside Conor. "That's bog iron."

"Bog iron?" Conor repeated.

"Sounds as though the lad knows the trade well fae one so young," a voice called from the glow of a large shed. The ringing of metal had ceased. "Not many knows bog iron on sight."

Conor turned towards the sound. Silhouetted against the glow of firelight within the nearest shed stood a burly giant. He took a step forward and Rhoyd gasped.

"Can I help ye?" the giant asked.

It was rare for Conor to meet a man taller than himself. This one was but a hair shorter than an opening that would have easily accommodated a dray horse. The giant possessed a golden mane of hair braided so that it coiled down his back. Stripped to the waist, he displayed a chest rife with burn and battle scars. His ruggedly handsome face sported the barest hint of a beard scuffing the square chin. But that handsomeness was betrayed by the lack of one eye. All that could be seen was an empty socket healed long ago. The remaining eye was the color of the bog iron clumps.

Conor cleared his throat. "I am Conor MacManahan. This is my wife Eithne, who is a True Healer, and that lad is my son Rhoyd. I am seeking one Whelan MacFee, and bring him greetings from his cousin the Laird of Heatherbloom.

A smile spread, softening the otherwise stern expression. "So, Angus sends me company, does he? Then come into my house and be welcome, for I am Whelan MacFee whom some men call Mad MacFee."

He stepped forward, offering Conor his hand. Smiling, Conor dismounted and took it. "And why is that?"

Whelan shrugged. "Who can say? My cousins will tell men that I appear mad to all who see me." He turned to look at Rhoyd with his one eye. "So ye know bog iron, do ye lad?" he asked.

Rhoyd nodded.

Whelan seemed to be studying Rhoyd in a hard way that made Conor wonder if the man was two-sighted. He once heard that men who lost one eye gained second sight. The smith stepped over and offered Rhoyd his hand in a gesture of welcome. Rhoyd hesitated, and then took it, only to have Whelan turn the hand over and study it.

"I know that scar," he said and touched one of the many that still faintly marked Rhoyd's hands. "You were a smith's apprentice once."

Rhoyd sighed and said softly, "I was a smith's son once, but no more. Conor is my father now."

Whelan nodded, glancing sideways at Conor. "Come into my house and be welcome, lad," Whelan said and grinned.

Rhoyd managed a smile that relieved the tension growing in Conor's gut. For there was something in that single eye that made Conor wonder if Whelan was mad after all.

The house was far neater than Eithne expected, but as soon as she was introduced to Whelan's wife, she understood why. A thickset woman of middle years, she was a formidable as her husband was tall.

"My cousin Angus has sent us guests, my dove," Whelan said as he led them into the kitchen of a two-story dwelling backed against his smithy.

Dove? There was nothing dove-like about Mistress MacFee. As soon as she saw the "guests," she glanced over her shoulder and shouted, "Moira, tell Lenore to make room for three more at the table. And tell your brothers iffen they dinna stop horsing around in the cellar and bring me them carrots, I'll add their fingers to the meat pies."

A pretty lass of nearly marriageable age nodded, putting aside the kneading of dough, and bolted from the kitchen.

"This is my wife, Onora MacFee, and that lass was our oldest daughter, Moira. My dove, this is Master Conor MacManahan and his wife Eithne who is a healer, and their son Rhoyd."

Onora pushed aside the knife she was using to turn large chunks of lamb into smaller ones and wiped her hands. "Welcome to our house. Forgive my appearance."

"Oh, there is nothing to forgive," Eithne said. "We are most grateful that you and your husband would allow us to share your roof and your meal. Is there anything I can do to assist?"

Mistress Onora smiled, losing the fierce look of a Keltoran black boar as she nodded. "Well, I could use a hand with the chopping of the carrots..." then added with a shout, "as soon as those hooligan sons of mine bring them up from the cellar."

As if by magic, a pair of boys, nine and eleven respectively, charged into the kitchen with bundles of carrots escaping from their arms. The lovely Moira was on their heels, flapping her apron as though shooing geese. She quickly went back to kneading the bread dough as the boys stopped and stared curiously at their visitor.

"Tam and Whelan the younger," their mother said, pointing to the youngest and the eldest. "We just call him Lan so we can tell him from his father."

Conor chuckled at that, and Master Whelan smiled with pride. Eithne bit her tongue rather than say that there was no resemblance between them other than the name. This was clearly some Keltoran humor that she was not familiar with.

Another lass slipped into the kitchen now, eyes wide with uncertainty. Need whispered from the child. She cast a furtive look at the newcomers then quickly headed for the corner cupboard to fetch more platters.

"And this is my sister's child, Lenora," Whelan said, stepping over to block her way before she could escape the room unseen. "She has come to live with us just the past fortnight as her parents walked into the Summerland."

"Oh, I am sorry to hear that," Eithne said as she handed her pack to Conor and crossed the room. "Are you ill, child?"

Whelan looked puzzled. "Ill?" he said and looked curiously at the lass. "Lenora, are you not well?"

The girl tensed, afraid to reply.

"I sense her need," Eithne said.

"Lenora has not spoken a word since she came to us after the loss of her mother and father, and we have yet to learn what became of them," Whelan said.

Lenora trembled as Eithne offered her own hand to the lass. Still, Lenora took it, and she quivered like a new colt as Eithne gently pressed her other hand to the child's forehead. *There is pain here, Blessed Brother,* Eithne thought. It was not unlike what she felt the first day she encountered and healed Rhoyd.

She must have witnessed something terrible, poor child.

"Perhaps she will tell you when she is able," Eithne said. She smiled and released the girl who looked expectantly at her uncle. Whelan nodded and stepped aside, and Lenora swiftly went to the cupboard, grabbing platters and fleeing the kitchen.

"Well, MacManahan, let me offer you an ale," Whelan said. "We'll let the women take care of their work and you can tell me news of the road and my cousin in Heatherbloom."

"'Twill be my pleasure," Conor said. Whelan grabbed two wooden mugs from the cupboard and took them over to a cask in one corner. Filling them, he guided Conor towards the hearth in the neighboring chamber, which was visible through the arches of the support beams. Beyond, Eithne saw stairs going up to the rooms above.

"Mother, can we play with Rhoyd?" Tam suddenly asked.

"If his mother says it's all right," Mistress Onora said.

"Oh, I am certain they will get on fine," Eithne said as she glanced inquiringly at Rhoyd. He nodded to show his approval and she smiled. It was rare on the road for him to get to be with lads and lasses near his own age.

She just hoped he would not be tempted to do something rash with his magic.

"You lads behave yourselves, then," Mistress Onora said. "Stay in the yard and don't go ambling about the streets."

"Come on," Tam said, clearly bolder than his elder brother as he caught hold of Rhoyd's arm. "We'll show you our father's forge."

The three of them sprinted, and for a moment, Eithne realized it was easy to forget because Rhoyd was mageborn that he was still a young lad. Shaking her head, she walked over to the worktable, picking up the hastily thrown bundles of carrots to clean and cut them apart.

"So, you and Master Whelan do not know how poor Lenora's parents died?" Eithne said.

Mistress Onora shook her head. "It was not a good death, I am certain. They lived alone in a croft not half a league from Coldforge. Over towards the Faolanwold. They had been here with Lenora just a few days before and gone back home late. Not two days later, a tinker comes round and tells of seeing things on the moors, wolves and the like. And of a farmstead that he stayed the night at where there was no one about. He described the house of my husband's kinswoman all too well for it to be any other, so Whelan and one of his cousins went out to see what had happened. They found Lenora locked in the cellar, but of her parents, the only sure sign was the stains of their blood. Whatever ravaged them fair tore the place apart, left nearly all in ruin."

"The lass was fortunate, then," Eithne said with a sigh. "No wonder the poor thing is afraid to speak."

"Depends on what one considers fortune, Mistress MacManahan. Whelan says she was like a wild thing when he found her, and it was a good thing he did, for she'd had naught but the root cellar's contents to keep her alive. He thinks perhaps her father and mother locked her down there to protect her as she has not spoken a word."

Eithne glanced at the lass who came creeping back in to claim a corner by the fire and her cousin. The girl Moirai held out a bit of the bread that was already baked and smiled. Lenora took it and smiled faintly back, then quickly began to devour it.

"I wish the Blessed Brother's gift allowed me to sift such bad memories from a child's mind," Eithne said, "Alas."

"Wolves, ye say?" Whelan said loud enough to distract her.

"Aye," Conor said. "I've ne'er seen so large a pack. They were like an army."

"I am sorry to hear that my cousin Angus lost his mother," Whelan said. "She was a good woman."

"Angus' mother is dead?" Onora said. "How?"

"We were given to understand that she had fallen from a great height," Eithne replied before Conor could. She was uncertain if it would be wise to mention what Rhoyd had been told by a spirit. "And that a wolf had eaten part of her."

She glanced towards Lenora. The child's eyes were wide with unnamed dread. She quickly looked down at her hands and closed her eyes as though fighting some terrible memory. She clenched one into a fist, and Eithne swore she saw a faint twinkle of white light form then vanish. Lenora opened the hand and sighed wistfully.

Then Moira quickly pushed a basket at her cousin and

said, "Here, while I finish kneading this why don't you fetch the eggs for me. And be mindful of the rooster. He's been testy lately."

Lenora looked relieved to have a reason to leave the room. She took up the basket and practically sprinted for the door.

Is the child is mageborn?

The girl was at the right age for such power to manifest. Eithne glanced at her host and hostess.

Did they know?

And would they be displeased to learn this was true?

She wished Rhoyd had not gone off to play with the other boys. He would know for certain.

Tam and Lan looked pleased when Rhoyd kept up with them as they raced from the house into the shed. Rhoyd stopped in the middle of the forge shed and took a deep breath. There was the warm smell of metal and hammer strikes, the musk of a man's sweat and something more. A sweet sort of bronze brightness, not so unlike the warmth of Conor's aura, swirled about the forge. The welcoming essence was in everything.

And there was power here as well. Rhoyd sensed it when they reached the heart of Coldforge, and now standing here in the smithy, he could feel a burn of magic.

What was it his father used to say about the melding of metals? That there was magic to it unknown to mortal men until after the time of the Great Cataclysm. Rhoyd had taken that for granted as a small lad, sitting in the forge watching his father stoke bellows and beat metal into everything from swords to horseshoes. But now as he stood in the middle of the shed, he could clearly feel magic.

Uncle Fenelon had spoken of forging magic into metal once, but when Rhoyd asked his Aunt Genna, she told him the art was forbidden.

"Ye can feel it, can't ye?" Lan suddenly said, moving around so he was looking at Rhoyd. "Yer one o' them, aren't ye?"

"One of what?" Rhoyd repeated cautiously, frowning at the boy who stood half a head taller and looked so much older.

"Mageborn," Tam quickly interjected, pushing his older brother aside and standing almost nose-to-nose with Rhoyd. "Da says that only mageborn can feel it."

Rhoyd hesitated then drew his shoulders back. "Yes, I am mageborn," he said and knotted one hand in a fist, ready to defend himself if he had to.

"Told ye," Tam said, punching Lan in the arm.

Lan punched back and all at once, the two of them were scuffling in the dirt. Rhoyd stood there watching, uncertain whether to try and stop them or just stay out of it. But then he felt a faint prickle down the back of his neck as though someone was trying to scry him. Startled, he turned towards the source.

The girl they had called Lenora was standing shyly at the opening of the shed. She stared intently at Rhoyd, frowning. He threw Tam and Lan another look, but they were too preoccupied with pummeling one another to notice, so he stepped over to the door. Lenora took a step back, clutching a basket of eggs, but did not flee.

"I can't feel you," she whispered so quietly, only he could hear her.

Rhoyd looked into her eyes. "I can feel you," he said. "You're..."

"Hey!" Tam shouted. "Lenora's making sweet eyes at Rhoyd."

"Better watch out or she'll put her bad eyes on you," Tam said.

They rushed over, jostling Rhoyd between them. He staggered then steadied himself by grabbing the frame of the door.

"Come on, if you can feel this place, you can feel the special place too," Tam insisted.

"The special place?" Rhoyd asked, momentarily

distracted from Lenora.

"The the cold forge," Lan said. "But we're not supposed to go there."

"Coward," Tam sneered. "You're a big bairn if you're afraid of an old stone."

"Da will hide us," Lan said.

"He needs to see it," Tam insisted. "That way we'll know if it's true."

"If what is true?" Rhoyd asked.

Tam smiled wickedly. "Our father is the *An Gobha Mor*, and he says the cold forge is haunted by the soul of the *An Gobha Mor* who forged the *Eigh Loisg* in the *fear teallach*. That is why father cannot use the cold forge to make weapons anymore."

Rhoyd almost reeled back. The *Eigh Loisg* was the name in his dream. The name spoken by the man who was facing the Shadow Lord.

"I want to see this place," he said.

"I want to see it too," Lenora said.

Tam and Lan turned to their cousin, mouths dropping open.

"So, she speaks after all," Lan said.

"Aye, but we won't let her come for she's a girl, and the magic of smiths is for men alone."

"Magic has no gender," Rhoyd said, remembering something his Aunt Genna was forever harping on. Uncle Fenelon said otherwise.

"But if we let her come, she'll tell Da," Lan said.

"If you don't let me come, I will tell him," Lenora said. "I will go and tell him now."

"She won't tell," Tam challenged. "She won't speak to Da because then he'll want to know what happened to her mum and da. She'll have to tell him that what she is caused her mum and da to disappear."

Rhoyd saw Lenora hesitate as though this news was sinking in. Her eyes moistened. "But I didn't make them disappear," she said miserably. "It was the beast."

"The beast?" Rhoyd said. "The wolf beast? A demon?"

Lenora looked at him and nodded. Rhoyd took a deep breath and turned to look at the brothers. "She has to come with us," he said. "She's like me."

The brothers traded looks and shrugged in a noncommittal manner. Lan walked away, heading for the far end of the smithy. Tam held his place and sneered at Lenora. "She won't come," he said. "Not when she sees the way."

He turned and marched over to join his brother at the far end of the smithy. Lan was kicking at the dirt and reeds that packed the floor at that end, and his exploration met a dull thump. Both Rhoyd and Lenora crept over as Lan knelt and brushed the reeds aside, revealing a ring and a bolt. He threw the latter open, and with Tam's help, he seized the ring and pulled.

A sigh of air rushed into the smithy, filled with the odors of damp earth and stone. Beneath it, Rhoyd sensed something as ancient as the world, a vague hint of cinnamon. He stiffened and saw Lenora's eyes go wide with fright. She glanced worriedly at him and whispered, "What's that smell?"

"Demon essence, I think," Rhoyd whispered back.

"Is it evil?"

Rhoyd took a deep breath and stretched mage senses. Using them like invisible fingers, he felt his way down a set of stairs cut into the stone below. The darkness yielded whorls of color and carvings to his probing.

"Demons made this path," he said softly. "But there are no demons down there now."

Tam and Lan had already started down into the dark, feeling their way along the wall as they descended. Rhoyd took a deep breath and offered Lenora his hand. She took it, her thin fingers strong as they latched around his. He could feel the quicksilver fire of mage essence within her. Nowhere near as strong as his grasp, it was still a comforting presence in a way. He tugged her hand and guided her to the edge. Together, they descended into the tunnel.

"Mind yer head," Tam called back.

Lan was grumbling against the dark. Rhoyd's mage eyes adjusted, revealing the artistry his senses had felt. The walls were carved and painted with whorls and figures.

The object of Tam's warning was a low beam of stone. Short as he was, Rhoyd and Lenora both had to duck under it. He wryly noted that she was not having any trouble negotiating this dark. While Lan and Tam were tripping over floor stones and bumping into walls, he smiled and glanced at Lenora. She put her free hand over her mouth to stifle a giggle.

The path went straight until the end when it twisted back on itself. Rhoyd rounded the corner, Lenora still close, and stopped. Here the corridor rose slightly. Tam and Lan were up ahead feeling around the walls that faced them.

"It's here somewhere," Tam said.

"We should have brought a lantern," Lan said.

"Fire won't burn down here," Tam said. "Da said so."

"What are you looking for?" Rhoyd asked, studying the pattern of colors on the wall they were fondling.

"A stone of yellow," Lan said, "painted with a dark red flame. But there is no way to see it in this dark."

"Like that one," Lenora said and releasing Rhoyd's hand, she pushed past the brothers and touched the yellow stone surrounded by a mosaic of blue and green.

Before they could reply, the stone slid inward and there was the hoarse grinding of stone moving against stone. Lenora hitched back behind Rhoyd as the walls opened, sliding apart.

"That's the one," Tam said, and putting his hand to the wall beside him, he started to step through.

And then he screamed and threw himself back, falling against Rhoyd.

"What is it?" Lan asked, flailing around with his hands in search of the danger.

Rhoyd staggered and regained his balance as Tam went skittering back the way they came on all fours.

"It's him!" he shrieked. "It's the *An Gobha Mor*! The Ancestor! He tried to strangle me."

A moaning sounded from just beyond the gap. Tam scrambled to his feet, hitting the wall and using it to bounce into the turn. Lan gave a yelp and whipped around, stumbling over Lenora before following his brother.

Lenora grabbed Rhoyd's hand. He stood still, peering into the dark beyond.

Something was fluttering in the wind, long threads of an ancient tapestry worn to near spider web density. The moaning would rise and fall in pitch, and with each flutter, the sound would waver.

It's only the wind, Rhoyd thought. He glanced back over his shoulder, but Tam and Lan were long gone.

"It's only the wind," he repeated aloud as he glanced at Lenora.

A smile fluttered across her lips. Lenora nodded. "The wind," she said, and her grasp on his hand lessened with relief.

Rhoyd stretched mage senses, and his probing was greeted with the kiss of ancient magic. He felt fire, stone, earth, and water, but none of these held any hint of darkness. So, he took a deep breath, slipping out of Lenora's waning grasp, and stepped into the opening. Stairs carved from the stone of the earth rose to a chamber above. Rhoyd climbed them until he had reached the level above.

Here was semidarkness, broken by a single flame of blue nestled in the heart of the forge.

How? he thought as he stepped closer to the old stone structure that had once been part of a very grand smithy. Looking around, he could see the implements of the trade, all carefully laid out as though waiting for an experienced hand.

But it was the flame that drew his attention the most. He stretched a hand towards it, and all he felt was a chill.

Cold fire? How was that possible?

"I think we should leave now," Lenora said. "I do not like this place."

"Why?" Rhoyd asked. "It's just a smithy."

"It feels like them," she said.

"Them?"

"The ones who came after my mother and father..." Lenora hesitated as though the words pained her.

"The ones who killed your parents?"

Lenora shook her head. " The ones who came after, they felt like my Uncle," she said. "What killed my parents was a monster. I only saw it briefly before my father pushed me into the cellar and barred the door. But it looked as though a wolf had mated with a demon. It was all fangs and claws and moved like a shadow. "

Rhoyd felt himself trembling. That sounded just like the creature he had seen in his dreams.

SEVEN

Two lads white-faced as winter snow pelted into the kitchen as though demons were on their heels. Conor had been sharing news of the road with Whelan, but the distraction of the noisy pair drew both their attention away from the tale. And Conor was first to note that Rhoyd was not among the pasty-faced pair.

Conor rose and fixing them with a hard stare asked, "Where's my son?"

They froze as one then looked sheepishly at their father who had also risen to his feet with a somber stare from his single eye. "Answer him, lads. What have ye done with yer guest?"

"The ghost tock him," Tam said, showing more pride than his elder brother who cowed. "Him and Lenora both."

"Ghost?" Conor said, glancing at Whelan.

The smith closed his one eye and sighed. "Did you take him there or did he find it on his own?" Whelan asked. He opened his eye again and glowered at his sons. "Well?"

"He..." Lan opened his mouth then froze and looked at the floor as what was clearly about to be a lie colored his cheeks. "We took him there. We wanted to see if he could see the Ancestor."

Tam reached around and poked his brother. "Coward," he muttered.

"I'll deal with ye later," Whelan said. "Ye know the rules. Bending them will only get ye a hiding."

"What are they talking about?" Conor asked. "What ghost? What ancestor?"

"Come, I know where they took him," Whelan said.

97

"You lads stay here with the women."

With that, Whelan started for the door. Tam and Lan stepped aside as though knowing their fate was sealed. Conor latched himself to Whelan's heels and followed the smith out into his shop.

Behind the anvil stand was an opening in the floor. Whelan shook his head and picked up a lantern. He touched the stone within it and whispered, *"Solus."* A bluish glow lit the way.

Howt awa, he's mageborn! Conor hesitated just a whit. Why hadn't he felt the magic in Whelan before? But if the smith noticed Conor's expression, he said nothing. Whelan descended stairs cut into the side of the hole. Concern for Rhoyd quickly overshadowed the unease. Conor stepped into the hole, following the smith closely.

The tunnel they entered had a bogie feel that made Conor's hair stand on end. "What is this place?" he asked.

"The Ancestor built it in times of darkness," Whelan said and gestured to the walls. "It was said he captured demons and forced them to cut the stonework."

"For what purpose?"

"You will see," Whelan said. "In the days of darkness when the Shadow Lord was master of everything within twenty leagues of the Faolanwold, a smith of the old way had to be careful. Watch out, the beam here is rather low."

So was the ceiling, Conor had noted, as both he and Whelan were forced to crouch as they walked the length of the hall. They trundled along for a long distance, then the hall took back on itself. The path sloped up to an opening and through them, stairs going up. Conor heard a moaning sound and saw in the light of the lantern that the walls moved. He had to duck under a low lintel. They started to climb when someone came rushing down the stairs.

There was a scream, a girlish sound, as the lass named Lenora ran into Whelan.

He caught her and stilled her cry with his hand.

"Where is he?" Whelan whispered.

She pointed up the stairs.

"Go back to the house," Whelan said. "I will talk to you later."

She fled past him and Conor. Whelan continued up the stairs, and Conor quickly moved up them as well, putting a hand to his dagger.

"Call to your son," Whelan said.

"Rhoyd?" Conor shouted.

There was a noise, sort of a cross between a "urk" and a "sigh."

"Rhoyd?" Conor called again.

"In here," the lad replied softly.

Conor relaxed, letting his hand fall from his hilt. He reached the top of the stairs now. Across the way, he made out a forge, and standing before it, silhouetted in blue light, stood Rhoyd.

"Are ye all right, lad?" Conor asked.

Rhoyd was not looking at him. The lad's gaze was on something up over his head. Conor turned to peer in that direction.

A hazy blue figure floated high in the air. It stared at Rhoyd with sad eyes and raised a finger to point at the lad.

"You see," it said. "And you know. And it knows you."

Conor started to drag out his sword, but Whelan's hand covered his hilt. The smith shook his head. "'Tis naught but a spirit," he said. "It has no power to do harm."

"The True Master will one day seek you out, Child of the Light," the spirit whispered. "And you must know the riddle of Ice and Fire, or you will be devoured and all hope will be lost."

Rhoyd did not move. The spirit faded to nothing in the blink of an eye, and only then did Rhoyd relax, leaning on the wall of the forge. Conor quickly crossed the floor to kneel before the lad.

"Are you hurt?" Conor asked.

Rhoyd shook his head, glancing cautiously at Whelan who set his blue-stoned lantern aside and came over to stand beside them.

"I'm sorry," Rhoyd said. "I shouldn't be here."

"My sons have already confessed to leading you here to see if you could see the Ancestor," Whelan said. "They have been told to stay out of this place because they are not what I am. But it is very clear that you are more than you seem, son of a smith no more."

Rhoyd cocked an eyebrow. "You're mageborn too," he said.

"Aye, as is my sister's child. But my sons possess no such skill. So, I shall have to pass my legacy on to the girl-child of my sister."

"Smith's magic," Rhoyd said.

"Aye. I am the last of the Keepers of The Ice Flame."

Conor rose. "You're the *An Gobha Mor?*"

"That I am. At least one of them. It was my ancestor who forged the *Eigh Loisg* that defeated the Shadow Lord of Dun Faolanwold. But for his part, he paid a terrible price--his life became forfeit. He had a son who possessed his power, and so it has been since the days of darkness, my kith and kin have held mastery over smith magic and tended the blue flame. I must pass that legacy on to one of my own bloodlines who has the power, but as you can see, the gods have chosen to give me two mischievous mortal born sons and placed the power in a woman's hands."

"But why?" Conor said. "Will the magic diminish in a woman's hands?"

"No," Rhoyd said quickly. "Power has no gender. Only in the way it is used."

"And the Balance of All Things decrees where the power lies," Whelan said. He reached out with one calloused hand and lifted Rhoyd's chin. "You are the Ard Magister, are you not?"

Rhoyd nodded. "So they tell me," he said.

"And you know the ways of a smith," Whelan said, releasing Rhoyd.

"Like I said, my father was a smith." Rhoyd said it with great reluctance, making Conor smile. He pushed a hand fondly through Rhoyd's hair.

"But you are not of my blood, so I cannot pass the knowledge on to you. But clearly, if you are the Ard Magister, then the Balance requires that a woman must be the *An Gobha Mor de Eigh*. And so, I will teach Lenora the ways of steel and fire and ice."

"But why did the Ancestor say that Rhoyd must master Fire and Ice to keep the dark from devouring him?" Conor asked.

"The Ancestor says many things of which we are never certain," Whelan said. "The Ard Magister may yet need to know the way of forging the weapons of the ancients. But the Keeper of the Blue Flame and its secrets will belong to my niece when the time comes. Remember her, Ard Magister. She will be your ally one day. Now, come, let us go back to the house so the womenfolk know that all is well."

Rhoyd hesitated, looking up at Whelan once more. "Are you going to punish Lan and Tam because of me?" he ventured.

Whelan shook his head. "They punish themselves more than I ever need to," he said with a half-smile and a wink.

"And Lenora?"

"I would cut my own throat before I would ever bring harm to her," Whelan said. "She is my future, even if she is not my son."

Rhoyd looked satisfied to hear this. "All right." He turned towards the blue flame, staring at it intently. "Just as long as you know she didn't hurt her family."

"I knew that the day I found her hiding in that cellar," Whelan said. "Now come. The women will think we have been eaten by bears."

"Inside a town?" Rhoyd said, looking at Conor first.

Whelan laughed. "He must be a handful at times," he said to Conor.

"That he is," Conor agreed. "But we love him anyway."

With that, Whelan laughed again, then turned and picked up the blue lantern. He led the way down the stairs and back into the tunnels. Conor followed, one arm around Rhoyd's shoulder.

He was glad to leave the bogie-feeling forge behind.

Eithne's first thought was to follow Conor when he and Whelan left, but she sensed no need. Only Conor's anxiety, which was more apparent in the way he moved, and in his expression, than any feeling she might have. She forced herself to wait in the house, continuing to slice vegetables for the pot while listening to Mistress MacFee.

"Those boys, I swear they will be the death of me," the smith's wife said as she savaged more chunks of mutton for the pot. "One minute they're little lambs, and the next I swear they are demon-get."

Eithne nodded. Her father had often said the same about Eithne's brothers.

Some moments passed, and her anxiety deepened. Perhaps she should have gone with the men. She was convinced that she should take off after them now, though she had no clue as to where they might be, when she heard the patter of footsteps, and looked up in expectation.

Lenora came slipping into the kitchen, looking rather pale. She quickly settled into a corner, and Eithne realized the lass did not have her basket of eggs.

Blessed Brother, what has happened? She glanced at Mistress MacFee to see if she had noticed. But she seemed more intent on her cooking. And then Moira came in, carrying the basket and looking a little put out. But she settled the basket next to Lenora who looked momentarily sheepish before she quickly began the task of sorting the eggs.

"Here, are you finished with them carrots?" Mistress MacFee suddenly asked, and her voice startled Eithne who nearly dropped the knife.

"Oh, yes," Eithne said, looking down at the mountain of vegetables before her.

"Then if you don't mind, throw them in the pot so this stew can start simmering."

Eithne nodded. She carried handfuls over to the pot of water already boiling over the fire and dumped them in. Three trips were required before the task was complete. Eithne dropped the last of the carrots in, then turned to the blacksmith's wife and said, "Now I think I shall go check on my husband and son."

Mistress MacFee looked up. "There's no need, Mistress MacManahan," she said. "Nothing is wrong, I can assure you. Tam and Lan just showed your son the smithy. No harm will come to him or your man. My Whelan will see to that. Now come here and stop fretting. We've a meal to get on, and the men folk are no help."

Eithne opened her mouth to protest when she heard voices from the doorway singing a familiar song.

"Oh, I hear the hammer ringing,
The anvil singing from within,
The smith is in his smithy,
And he's making such a din,
He'll wake the men from Bonny Bough
Up to the Ferlie Glen..."

"Blessed Brother," she muttered and turned in time to see Whelan and Conor come in with Rhoyd between them. All of them were bellowing the chorus as they stopped in the center of the kitchen. Mistress MacFee put down her knife and clapped her hands with glee.

"Oh, I haven't heard ye sing that in ever so long," she said. "What handsome voices your men folk have, Mistress MacManahan. We shall surely have to have song and dance after our meal."

"I have pipes as well," Conor said, and Eithne clamped down the protest that bubbled through her thoughts, knowing it would only be an insult to their host and hostess.

"I just hope your neighbors are forgiving," she muttered.

Conor looked at her and winked. "All is well, woman," he assured her. "The lads were just larking about, and no one was hurt."

She sighed rather than express her thoughts. "If you say so," she said instead and turned to the task of stirring the pot just to keep him from seeing the livid color that rose in her cheeks.

Still, he came over and wrapped arms around her. "These are good people, Eithne," he whispered to reassure her.

She nodded, continuing her task, and letting him catch but a glimpse of her smile.

The rest of the evening went well, she was pleased to note. In due course, the meal was finished. Conor dragged out his pipes afterwards, and Whelan produced a chanter, and between them, a cacophony of songs ensued. Moira was adept at playing harp, and Tam had learned to beat a bodhran. Mistress MacFee danced a jig with her eldest son. Eithne sat on the bench and clapped to keep time.

But as she sat, she could not help noticing Rhoyd and Lenora over by the fire. Had she missed something, she wondered. They were ignoring the noise. Rhoyd's lips moved, and Eithne saw a wad of light appear around his hand. He turned it into a sphere and held it out to Lenora. She took it and it did not die in her hands as Eithne had seen it do when he handed it to others.

She is mageborn...

Eithne glanced over at Conor. The set had finished, and he was taking a quaff of ale. MacFee stood up and announced that he would sing The Raven's Lamentation. Conor caught her glance and followed the direction of her gaze when she shifted it. He smiled and put the pipes aside and walked over to sit with her.

"He's showing her magic," Eithne said. "Should he…"

"I told ye, woman, these are good people. The lass is mageborn as is our host, and he says when the time comes, he will be showing her the secrets of the *An Gobha Mor* because neither of his sons are mageborn."

Conor said it in such a matter-of-fact way that Eithne fixed him with a hard stare.

"What?" he said. "Ye should be pleased. Lads his age are usually shy around her gender. I remember trying to hide in the stables the first time a lass that age came at me. It's a wonder I was able to face you when I was a man."

"Oh, so now you're planning to marry him to the first girl who does not frighten him?'

"I ne'er said anything of the sort, woman," Conor retorted. "But ye've no cause to get yer breeches in a twist. There be nothing wrong with him showing her the glamorie. Better than what he could be showing her."

A leering grin spread across Conor's face.

"You…" Eithne frowned and punched him in the arm, and then leaned against him as Whelan's voice boomed out the sad ballad.

"The raven wheeled across the moors
A battle fierce its eyes did see.
Scores of men clashing arms
Against the enemy…

The Shadow Lord has come again
To spread his curse across the land
The Shadow Lord has come to hear
The raven's lamentation…"

Eithne tried not to frown. What a terribly grim song, she thought as Whelan sang of darkness and destruction and the near end of all humankind, and of a raven that wheeled about the battlefield, feeding on the dead.

Keltorans! Why are their older songs so dark? To Eithne's dismay, Rhoyd stopped showing Lenora how he could roll light spheres around on his hands and started listening. His face grew stoic as the song drew to a close.

"They say another Shadow Age,
Shall come upon the world of men
And when it does, the Dark will rise
To hide the world in night.

And should the one Twice-Blooded born
Be unprepared in ways of old
The Shadow Lord will live again
And take away the light..."

Silence fell like a heavy wool blanket, muffling all sound.

"That wasn't very cheerful," Eithne said with a frown.

Conor winced, but Whelan merely smiled.

"It has never been a song to cheer the heart, I will confess," the smith said. "I learned it from my father when I was no older than my sons, and it gave me nightmares."

"Small wonder," Eithne said.

She glanced at Rhoyd who had gone back to showing Lenora how to write glyphs on the air.

And could not help wondering just how much of that terrible song was about him.

Ensconced in the pallet next to the fire, Rhoyd slept like he had not done in so long. When he rolled over on his back and opened his eyes, he was surprised to see the barest hints of dawn peeping through the shutters. He turned his head so he could see if Conor and Eithne were still abed and discovered them sleeping soundly.

Good, I didn't wake them up--or anyone else for that matter. Perhaps he had been tired from horsing around with Tam and Lan, for even though he had spent as much time as he could showing Lenora magic and teaching her basic cantrips, he had equally gotten caught up with racing about the smithy yard like a hooligan.

Strange, his real mother had never allowed him to run and play with others his own age. She always feared Rhoyd would do or say something to give his mageborn skills away and reveal to the elders of the Temple of Cromm the Savior that one they called enemy lived among them. Rhoyd had never been able to bolt about with abandon, throw rocks at old stumps or wrestle. Granted, his real father had often tried to roughhouse with him, but mother always hovered at the edges, terrified that something would go wrong, and Rhoyd came to dread those moments because Evan had not been a gentle man.

Rhoyd was no weakling, he told himself. Working in the smithy had given him a sinewy body, capable of enduring much. He'd had to endure a lot. Otherwise...

He pushed the thoughts away. The past was gone. His father was dead, nothing more than dust among the darker memories of Rhoyd's youth. Indeed, there were times he thought he had forgotten that there was another father in his life besides Conor.

But here in the familiar aura of the smithy of Whelan MacFee, some memories were being stirred. Was it the distant din of a hammer ringing?

Pushing his covers aside, Rhoyd sat up and found his stockings, trews and boots and pulled them on. He snatched up the bit of plaidie he now called his own. Pulling it about his shoulders for warmth, he quietly slipped out of the chamber.

There were sounds in the kitchen, a woman humming a soft familiar tune. Rhoyd peered through the doorway and spied Mistress MacFee hard at work with the help of her daughter and Lenora. Life clearly had to go on. He watched her for a moment then moved on, heading for the sound of the hammer.

Out in the yard, Tam and Lan loaded a small handcart

with wheels.

"Now mind you lads get those straight to the carter, and then get yersels back here," Whelan said called from inside the smithy. "No larking about, ye hear?"

Tam and Lan grabbed their handcart and shoved it through the gate, not even noticing Rhoyd standing in the doorway watching them leave. He sighed and wandered over to the forge shed, glancing at the grey sky.

"Hoi, I see yer up and about," a booming voice sounded from within.

Rhoyd peered through the opening into the smithy. It looked different in the daytime. Less threatening in many ways. Whelan stood by his forge, thrusting a shaft of metal in and out of the coals.

"Are ye gonna watch from there, laddie, or will ye be coming in?" Whelan asked.

"I don't want to get in the way," Rhoyd said.

"Yer a smith's son, so I rather doubt ye would get in the way."

Rhoyd pulled his plaidie tighter. "I haven't been a smith's son in a long time," he said as he stepped on into the shed and seated himself on an old bench that was little more than a large log with flattened sides. The surface wore a thousand scars from metal scoring. His father had one, and Rhoyd had known it too well. His stomach hurt with the memory of being held down over that rough surface and beaten with traces.

Rhoyd pulled his knees to his chest and tried not to remember. But in doing so, he looked up and saw the sad pity in Master Whelan's eyes.

"Ye had the look of a bad thought there, lad," Whelan said.

Rhoyd shrugged. "What are you making," he asked, hoping to sway the conversation elsewhere.

"'Twill be a spear soon," Whelan said. "Been working on it most of the night. Some forging is best done at night so no one sees. Come look."

Rhoyd crawled off the bench and approached, peering into the coals. Heat lapped his face and made him catch his breath. But he drew nearer and investigated the red depths.

The metal was blue, despite the heat. The haft was longer than Rhoyd thought necessary for a spearhead. He peered at it, and as he did, he saw the marks on its surface. Runes.

He glanced warily up at Whelan. "I thought mixing magic and metal was forbidden," Rhoyd whispered.

Whelan smiled. He drew the spearhead out with his tongs and thrust it into the water trough. The squealing hiss of metal smoked the air and lent it a familiar metallic odor.

"Why are you putting that in water?" Rhoyd asked. "Won't that make it brittle?"

"Yer a smart lad," Whelan said and winked his one eye. "That water comes from under the Cold Forge. Comes from a spring deep in the earth that we call *Uisge Draioch*, a gift from the Lord of Water himself that only the *An Gobhar Mor* may use. It's magic water?"

"What would happen if you drank it?" Rhoyd asked.

Whelan laughed. "Ye'd go mad just like me."

Rhoyd scried the water, feeling the power in it. He watched as Whelan whisked the spearhead around. Steam rose as the smith drew the blade from the trough and laid it on the anvil.

"Touch it," Whelan said.

Rhoyd hesitated, looking up at the smith of Coldforge as though he had grown horns and a tail. *Maybe he has been drinking the magic water,* Rhoyd thought.

"There's naught to fear," Whelan insisted. "You know how."

Rhoyd cocked an eyebrow. He took a deep breath and whispered, *"Cha loisg mi,"* as he cautiously placed a hand on the haft.

The metal was cold as though it had been stored in ice. And magic swirled about it. Rhoyd stared as tendrils of white fire, little tongues of flame licking his skin, crawled back and forth over the surface. Some vague sense of familiarity rose. Where had he seen this before?

"Ice Fire," he said and smiled as he looked up at Whelan.

"Aye," Whelan said. "Yours for the taking."

"What?" Rhoyd reared back.

"I'll fit it to a short shaft suited to your size. And when you're older, bring it back and I'll make it fit you as a man."

"But I can't take this."

Whelan reached for Rhoyd's hand and pulled it down on the blade. "You are going to need this, lad. One day, this may be all that stands between you and the Dark Mother's champion. Take it as a gift from me, a gift of gratitude."

"For what?"

Whelan glanced towards the door. Rhoyd turned to look that way and spied Lenora entering the forge. She had tucked her skirt up like a pair of baggy trews and had her hair pulled back in a braid.

"For giving her a voice again," Whelan said. "Because now I can teach the ways of the *An Gobha Mor* and make her heir to my ways."

Lenora smiled shyly and stepped on into the shed.

"Now go. I sense that yer father may be rising. The spear will be ready when you leave."

He released Rhoyd's hand. Rhoyd drew back and with a glance at Lenora, he hurried out of the smithy.

"All right, me merry maid," he heard Whelan say cheerfully. "Are ye ready to learn the true secrets of steel?"

"I am, Uncle," Lenora replied.

"Then let's find a proper bit of good ash wood to set this spearhead in for the Ard Magister, and then we'll start ye to work."

The rest of the conversation was lost as Rhoyd stepped back into the cottage.

EIGHT

Conor continued to eye the staff Whelan presented to Rhoyd just as they were leaving Coldforge that morning. As he walked Battlebrute along the moor road, he tried not to stare directly at it, but he could see it from the corner of his eye where it was slung off Rhoyd's saddle. Little Moonface didn't seem to mind the staff thumping against his flank, and Rhoyd was too preoccupied with one of his books to notice. But Conor would not allow himself to embarrass the lad by staring. Besides, the moor was becoming more forested, and a man could not afford to be anything but vigilant in such a place.

That spear seemed a fancy bit of work, just to be giving it away. Conor wanted to refuse. It wasn't natural for a host to give gifts to guests, unless it was food for the journey--which Mistress MacFee had made certain they had. That, Conor gladly took. But the short spear? At first, Conor thought it was a staff of ash with a dragon coiled about the top, but Whelan revealed how the knotwork-covered wooden beastie's bronze claws could be unlatched from the metal ring at its base by giving it a half turn, and when it slid free, it revealed the gleaming steel beneath.

Howt awa! Conor might not be one of the mageborn, but he could see the faintest hint of a glow dancing along the sharp edge. And he knew that those marks etched into its surface were more than decoration. He'd seen enough of the runes and warding marks to know them on sight. When he dared to touch the steel, the brush of a breeze across the backs of his hands made him shiver. There was bogie magic in the thing.

Horns! From what Conor could see, Rhoyd seemed delighted for it to be there.

"He'll be cutting his toes off," Conor muttered.

"Then you must teach him the way of it," Whelan replied.

He refused to accept payment, which bothered Conor more than anything. Granted, he could not part with the princely sum such a weapon would have normally demanded, but he thought some sort of compensation was due. Whelan shook his head.

"It is my place in the Balance of All Things to make this for him," Whelan insisted. "And when he grows taller, bring him back to get a new shaft for it. If I am no longer here, the girl will make it for him."

Conor shook his head. He would make certain somewhere along the way that some repayment was made. And when they stopped for brief breaks along the road, he'd take time to show Rhoyd how to use his deadly stick.

For now, Conor decided he'd best keep his attention on this road. The trees were still thin enough that a man could see a fair clip. Large scatterings of stones were everywhere. This part of Keltora was sheep country. Too rocky to graze cattle well--not that men didn't do it. As they passed a couple of pastures on the outskirts of Coldforge occupied by shaggy Keltoran cattle with the wide-set horns, the beasts would look up unconcerned, and then go back to grazing.

The party rode on in silence, passing more stones, more trees. As the day wore on, Conor realized that he didn't feel as tired as before. He had slept well last night. Rhoyd had not suffered his dreams under Whelan's roof.

For that, Conor had been grateful. He felt more alert and alive.

And it was a good thing, or he would not have noticed that when the road wound into a turn, that there were tracks across the ground.

Small tracks.

Conor drew rein and raised a hand. Rhoyd and Eithne quickly complied.

"What it is?" Eithne asked.

Conor motioned for silence. He surveyed the turn ahead. It did have the look of a bandit's favorite roost. But it was the tracks that had him puzzled. They were too small for grown men--or even women. And mingled with them, the familiar paws of more than one large canine.

Wolf tracks?

Never taking his eyes off their surroundings, he leaned towards Rhoyd.

"Do ye sense anyone, lad?" he asked.

Rhoyd closed his eyes briefly. Frowning, he shook his head.

"There's no one here but us," the lad said.

"Are ye certain?" Conor asked and gestured to the ground.

The faintest flicker of recognition flitted through those blue eyes.

"There's no one here but us," Rhoyd repeated. "I swear. We're alone at this moment."

Conor sighed.

"All right, lad, if yer certain," he said. "But I don't like the look of this. Something doesn't feel right to me and that's too good of an ambush spot ahead. You two stay back here until I signal all clear."

Rhoyd nodded. Eithne moved Maudie up so that she was beside the lad. Conor nudged Battlebrute into a walk. The old warhorse stepped on without hesitation, leaving Conor to wonder if his unease was necessary. One hand braced on the hilt of his sword, ready to draw it free, Conor guided his horse around the curve.

The stones here were close to the road, creating a natural wall as the road descended. The perfect place for a bandit to hide--or a predator waiting for small prey. The hairs were rising on the back of Conor's neck. How could the lad say there was no one about? Conor had the feeling something was watching him from close by. He twisted back and forth, then looked topside. In the shadows of the small tree growing there, he swore he saw the shadow of a wolf and the glitter of feral eyes, but both vanished in a blink.

What in the name of Cernunnos? He forced Battlebrute to the opposite side of the trail, hoping for a better look, but if something--or someone--had been there, they were gone now.

He glanced back and realized from this angle, he could see Rhoyd. The lad was peering studiously into the forest. Beside him, Eithne waited patiently at the head of the turn. With a sigh, Conor released his sword and motioned for them. They punched their heels into their horses and followed, looking relieved.

Conor turned one more glance at the rise, hoping to see something, but there was nothing.

And the bogie feeling of being watched had vanished as well.

The sun was angling towards the west when Eithne felt the burn of need so strong she nearly choked.

"Conor!"

Conor stopped abruptly, glancing back as she scanned the forest beyond the clearing below them. The trees there were thicker, creating deep shadows.

"What is it, woman?" he asked, riding back to her side.

"There is need here," she said and pointed. "Over there. Down in that forest."

"Let me lead, will ye," he said. "Rhoyd, get yer nose out of that book lad, and stay by me."

Rhoyd snapped shut the small tome he had been perusing, and with a practiced hand, he slipped it into his pack and put heels to Moonface to ride after Conor who cantered down the slope towards the tree line and then drew his mount down to a walk as he reached the edge.

Eithne took the rear, eager to reach the source. She felt such an abundance of need it was making her sick. She had not felt such a powerful need since the days of the Last War. The overwhelming pain and suffering nearly tumbled her from her horse even now, but she clung fiercely, knowing that the Brother's will and her skill were to be put to the test.

Conor picked the path of least resistance to enter the depth of the trees. Battlebrute danced under him, either from nervousness or eagerness. Conor kept one hand tight on the reins and the other slipped his sword from his scabbard. Eithne saw Rhoyd put a hand to his spear as though he knew how to use it, and she felt just as impelled to reach for her staff.

They broke into a clearing where a massacre had taken place. Weary farm folk looked up from tending their own wounded. The odor of blood and death fouled the air.

"Howt awa," Conor muttered. "What happened here?"

A couple of men holding hoes and staffs wandered over to stand at a wary distance. "If you are bandits come to take what little is left to us, know that we will fight to the last man," one of their eldest snarled.

Eithne quickly rode forward. "We mean you no harm," she said. "I am Eithne Manahan, a healer of Diancecht, and this is my husband and my son. I felt your need and have come to answer in the Blessed Brother's name."

"You're a True Healer?" one of the women cried.

"That I am," Eithne said.

There was a clamor all around. "My son...my husband...my child...my wife..." Eithne did not wait for Conor to say the word. She quickly dismounted and dragged her pack from the back of the saddle. Leaving Maudie to graze, Eithne hurried into the carnage, knowing the mare was too stupid to react to anything.

As Eithne darted off, Conor re-sheathed his sword and dismounted. "You stay in the saddle, lad," he said, "and keep a sharp eye out."

Rhoyd nodded. Conor turned back to the old farmer who approached him.

"You, sir, can ye tell me who did this?" Conor asked

The farmer relaxed.

"Halwn is my name," the farmer said. "And the same thing that drove us from our homes did all that you see. 'Twas no man, though, but a shadowy beast with a hunger."

Conor frowned and glanced back at Rhoyd to make certain the lad was staying alert. "What sort of beast?" Conor said.

Halwn took a deep breath. "It looked like a wolf, my lord, but no wolf I have ever seen can walk upright like a man. It looked more like a thing that had escaped from a tomb. It tore through our camp like a storm, and then just fled as though it had been summoned away."

Conor sighed, glancing around. He saw Eithne moving about, stitching, bandaging, and healing the living. But there looked to be just as many dead lying around.

"What should we do now, my lord?" Halwn asked.

It was on the tip of Conor's tongue to tell the man that he was no lord. Instead, he gestured to one of the corpses. "Best we get to either burying or burning yer dead," Conor said. "Otherwise, there will be more predators. I'll help ye, whichever way ye wish to deal with them."

Halwn nodded, looking relieved to have some one else in charge. "Yer right, my lord. Burning might be best. 'Twill hopefully keep the predators at bay."

"Sir, I am no lord," Conor said. "Just a mercenary who has been to war."

"That makes ye a better leader than I," Halwn said with a bob of his head.

He hurried away to must enough folks to gather wood and build a pyre for the dead. It wasn't easy, what with some of the corpses barely holding together. Soon enough, they had the fire going. The odor of charred flesh wafted through the air.

Once the dead were dealt with, Conor changed his focus. This was not a good place to stay. He approached Halwn once more, pulling him aside.

"We need to drag yer camp out onto the road," Conor said. "There are too many shadows here for a beast to hide in."

"But up there, bandits will see us," Halwn said.

"Do yer fear bandits more than what did all this?" Conor asked.

Halwn hesitated, then nodded. "Yer right, my lord," he said. "We shall do as ye ask."

In due order, with everyone able pitching in, the camp, their carts, and what remained of their livestock were moved up onto the open stretch of road just above the wood. Conor showed them how to set up defenses. He saw Eithne assisting the women in the preparations of a meal and jostling crying bairns. All the while, Rhoyd remained on Moonface's back, watching like a sentry.

"When it gets dark," Halwn argued, "then what? The beast attacks at night, in the shadows. We set watch fires last night, and it found its way into our midst and did all that you saw."

Conor sighed and glanced over at the rest of the farmer folk. "How do ye feel about mageborn, sir," he asked.

Halwn arched eyebrows and shrugged. "I would give anything if there were one here among my kin, for I am certain we would not have been attacked as we were."

Conor nodded. "Rhoyd, come on down now, lad."

Rhoyd dismounted, still holding his spear with the dragon hiding the point. Solemnly, he walked over to where Conor and Halwn stood.

"This is my son, and he is mageborn," Conor said. "I will have him put marks of protection all around the camp. The beast will not come inside those."

Halwn nodded, looking relieved.

Rhoyd didn't like the stink of blood that the air held. Nor the scent of death whose essence filled the woods, so he was glad at least to be up here on the road. Stifling his unease, he had done as Conor instructed and walked the widest perimeter around the camp and set up marks of warding. It took nearly an hour, and the sun had almost set by the time he finished. A circle of warm light glowed pale for the moment. He knew it would be stronger as dark fell.

He only hoped it would work against the demon.

Once the circle was set, the farmers settled down in a huddle around the fires. Conor had insisted they draw their wagons together to make a defensible place. Now, they gathered together like so many rabbits, shoulder to shoulder in a nest, looking miserable.

"We are grateful, my lord, that your son has such admirable skills," the old man named Halwn said.

"You said that the beast that drove you from your home is the same that slaughtered your kith and kin last night?" Conor said.

"Aye, that it was. Our farmstead is but another league from here, and two leagues from the edge of the Faolanwold, and we were fine there until the beast came. It plagued us nightly, and then it came into our homes and killed many of my family. A fire was started in one of the barns, and much was destroyed in the blaze. We had no choice but to leave."

"This beast clearly has a far reach," Conor said, rubbing his chin in thought.

Rhoyd caught the brief flicker of Conor's glance when it strayed in his direction.

"I have heard tales of it causing trouble as far away as Heatherbloom," Halwn said with a nod. "We've had travelers stay over at our farm before the trouble began to plague us and heard them speak of the thing. Folks who live at the base of Ben Faolan have been barring their doors, but that does not seem to stop this monster. They fear it has come to bring back the old darkness from the days before the Great Cataclysm."

"Aye, well, I think that men should not be so quick to fear the worse," Conor said.

Rhoyd bit his tongue rather than speak. He wished he were holding his spear, for it gave him a certain sense of security, but it lay beside him on the ground. Picking it up might make Conor think Rhoyd was sensing something.

Darkness grew deeper among the trees. At length, the farmers began to retire, though there was talk of setting watches. Especially when the faint yipping sounds of wolves far away echoed in the dark. Rhoyd knew he would not be able to sleep, but he crawled into his pallet near one of the fires all the same. He closed his eyes and pretended to fall asleep.

In time, snoring filled the air. Rhoyd barely opened his eyes. He could see Conor standing by the centermost fire, one hand on his sword, gazing out into the dark.

Horns, Rhoyd thought. How could he meet the Fearfaolan if Conor was awake? Cautiously Rhoyd tried to stretch mage senses, and as he did, he saw Conor turning his way, so he broke off the attempt and closed his eyes. He heard Conor crossing the ground, stopping close by, exuding the bronze warmth of his essence so that it wafted over Rhoyd. The creak of leather and dull clink of muffled chainmail were closely followed by the weight of a hand gently touching him. Rhoyd gasped, startled by the motion, and opened his eyes.

"It's just me, lad," Conor said. "Didn't mean to wake ye. Just thought I felt something."

Rhoyd sat up and pretended to knuckle sleep from his eyes. "What was it?" he asked.

"Well...it felt a wee bit like your magic," Conor said.

Rhoyd frowned. "I was just...checking," he said carefully.

"For what?" Conor asked.

Rhoyd sighed. "To make sure it wasn't out there."

"Is it?" Conor asked.

Rhoyd closed his eyes and concentrated, taking

advantage of the moment to touch the world and seek essence. He felt the familiar essence of the Fearfaolan. They were waiting for him, along with their wolves. Rhoyd opened his eyes and shook his head.

"The beast isn't out there," he said.

"Good," Conor said. "Because I am about dead on me feet and need to sleep."

"Surely, it won't come near us," Rhoyd said. "There's too much light."

Conor nodded. "In that case, I believe I will take a bit of a nap."

"I could stand watch for you," Rhoyd offered.

Conor grinned and tapped Rhoyd's nose. "Kind of ye to offer, lad, but I think you look as tired as I feel. Now you go back to sleep."

Rhoyd nodded and lay down on his pallet, closing his eyes. He listened as Conor moved over to the pallet where Eithne slept. Rhoyd barely opened his eyes again, peering through his thick lashes at the silhouette of Conor. He removed his sword, but not his armor, and lay down beside Eithne. Then he closed his eyes.

Rhoyd waited, counting his own heartbeats until at last he heard the familiar burr of Conor sleeping. Cautiously, Rhoyd pushed his blankets aside and rolled to his knees. He picked up his spear and stole quietly over to the edge of camp. The Fearfaolan were down in the forest waiting for him. No one stirred as he stepped through the circle of flames, snatching a bit of the light in his hand to carry with him. It left a flickering trail of fireflies in his wake as he swiftly made his way towards the woods.

The air still lingered with the stench of scorching flesh and bone as he slipped into the trees. But he also detected the animal muskiness of the Fearfaolan and their wolves. Mage eyes picked up the shift in the shadows and revealed forms crouching therein. He stopped in the middle of the clearing filled with death and waited.

The first to emerge from the trees were the wolves that had carried Rhoyd back to the cottage that night. Brown Chaser boldly walked up to Rhoyd and pushed his head under Rhoyd's hand. The she-wolf Wind Sidhe came more slowly, accompanied by Greymoon. Then other members of the clan, Fearfaolan and their wolves, moved into the clearing and crouched in a circle. A few of them turned to watch outward like sentries.

"This isn't going to take long, is it?" Rhoyd asked. "If Conor wakes up and finds me gone..."

Greymoon's lupine features stretched into the semblance of a smile. "I see you have the spear," she said.

"The *An Gobha Mor* gave it to me," Rhoyd said.

"Good, for it will be of service to you," she said.

She squatted and gestured for Rhoyd to do the same. He cast mage senses briefly up the hill to make sure he was not being missed. Then he settled on his haunches in a place she pointed to. With one hand, she cleared a spot in the dust, drawing a circle with one finger. He realized that her other hand clutched what looked like a cudgel shaped like a claw.

"This is how it began," she said. She reached into her pouch and drew forth a set of stones, planting them around the edge of the circle. Rhoyd sensed the magic in them, and as he watched her pass her hand over the circle in a sun wise motion, the space between glittered and shifted and formed a shimmering mirror. "The Shadow Lord came from the depths of the earth one day, the son of the Dark Mother and one of her elderkin, half demon, half dragon, with a soul as black as the pits of Annwn. They called him Dubh Sealgair, the Black Hunter, and his greatest delight was to follow his hounds to the destruction of every man and beast that dared to oppose him.

"He built himself a keep atop our mountain, and from there, he sent his mother's darkness over the land.

"To assist him in his rule, the Dark Mother gave him a disfigured beast she had formed by mating one of her demons to a wolf, the beast we know as Cu' Deamhan, and such a hideous thing it was. For not all her Shadow Lords were fearsome to behold. Dubh Sealgair was handsome in his own dark way. In fact, the only way one knew of his blood was by his eyes, which were all black and glowed with a most unnatural light under the shadow of night. The beast that became his right hand was large as a pony and terribly deformed. Sometimes it walked on all fours. Sometimes, it stood upright like a man. Always, it carried the stench of the tomb.

"The first thing that Dubh Sealgair did was to send the Cu' Daemhan out to slay our kind. For we are children of the White One, her creations from the earliest days of the world. Those of us he did not slay, he sought to subdue. He took our females captive and bred them to his followers, determined to wipe out our blood.

"It was said that one of our females was so beautiful, that he took her for his own. She was Cath Mathair whose name meant War Mother. We are by nature a peaceful race, but even a peaceful race must have protectors. War Mother and her Pack were our guardians. When Dubh Sealgair came, she and her Pack met him and his dark kin in battle. It was a fierce fight and War Mother's pack did kill a goodly number of the dark kin. But there were far too many of them, and soon she and her Pack were overwhelmed. Dubh Sealgair killed the rest of her Pack, but he took her as his slave.

"And he took her to his bed where he swiftly learned that a bitch of our kind is not easily swayed. He forced himself on her again and again, and then left her for dead.

"What he did not know was that one of our healers was also in his keep as a slave, and that one helped War Mother to escape and took her far away to be healed. And soon, it was discovered that Dubh Sealgair's seed had taken hold in her. The healer offered to kill the seed, but War Mother said no. We do not kill children because of their fathers.

"Instead, she went into the deepest mountains of the north to let her belly swell, and there she gave birth to the seed of Dubh Sealgair. He did not look Fearfaolan. Oh, no, he looked just like his father, a handsome man-kin, but instead of eyes as black as pitch, his were gold like the dawn. The eyes of Fearfaolan. She named him Banfaolan.

"War Mother raised him as a man-kin, taught him her battle ways and her secret ways as well. And when he was of age, she called the White One to look favorably on him then sent him back to the Dun of the Faolan to face his father.

"They say that a fierce battle was waged on that very spot. And aided by the secret ways and battle ways of his mother, Banfaolan defeated Dubh Sealgair and trapped him in the stone at the heart of the keep.

"There was still the demon beast Cu' Deamhan to reckon with, and it fought with Banfaolan as well and wounded him sorely. Before Banfaolan succumbed to his wounding, he sealed the beast into the cave at the heart of Ben Faolan. The White One then sent her Champion to seal all entrances to those caves, and so the darkness slept.

"And there it would have remained until the next turning of the Balance of All Things, but somewhere in the world, the blood of a mageborn was shed upon a gateway of stone. That blood seeped through the cracks and opened one of the gates. And so it was, the tomb at the heart of Ben Faolan was cracked, and the beast was set free.

Brina, Rhoyd thought. She set it free.

"Now, it must be returned to that grave for the time of the turning is not yet at hand. The shadows are gathering too soon. The An Gobha Mor gives you the Ice Fire because you will face the Darkening one day. But until the proper time comes, you must restore the beast to its prison."

"Restore it to its prison?" Rhoyd stepped back. The

mirror of Greymoon's making faded.

"Aye," she said and gathered her stones and placed them back in her sack. "Else wise, the darkness of the old days will return before its time. The beast will set the Dubh Sealgair free, and he is a foe you are not yet ready to face."

"But how can I put the beast back?"

"You have the spear Ice Fire," she said. "It was Ice Fire the burned the beast into the stone. It is Ice Fire that will put the beast back again, but only if you have the courage to face the beast in the tower atop Ben Faolan."

"But we're not going to Ben Faolan," Rhoyd said. "We're heading for the Faolanwold, and into the mountains and..."

"The road you seek will take you past the trail that leads to the keep," she said. "There you will find an archway of walking stones to shorten your road. And fear not, for the Fearfaolan will be with you. Brown Chaser and Wind Sidhe will be there at your bidding. I shall come when the moment is right. You will not be alone."

Rhoyd sighed. Several of the Fearfaolan had already slipped away. Brown Chaser and Wind Sidhe pushed close to him like lapdogs wanting his attention.

"Then I best get back to camp before Conor sees that I am gone," Rhoyd said. He petted the wolves and started to turn away.

But Brown Chaser's hackles rose, and Wind Sidhe crouched as though ready to attack. Rhoyd froze as a shadow came slipping out of the woods...

A black wolf with eyes of fire--a creature what exuded the essence of a demon--now stood between Rhoyd and the way back to the safety of camp.

"Shadow wolf!" Greymoon shouted, then threw back her head and howled.

The wolf howl from such close quarters jerked Conor out of his sleep. He reached for his sword as he sat up on the pallet. Around him, others stirred, and a babe whimpered then wailed. Frightened mutters grew in volume.

"It has come again," someone hissed.

Eithne opened her eyes, muttering, "Whuh..."

Conor glanced over towards Rhoyd's pallet and was greeted with empty blankets.

Horns!

He clambered to his feet, looking around, hoping--praying--the lad was safe inside the circle of light, but there was no sign of that black-hair bobbing anywhere among the tows and browns and auburns that surrounded him. Conor filled his lungs with air and shouted, "Rhoyd!"

All hopes were dashed when the wolf call was answered by a dozen more. The farmers began to cry out in alarm, and at once, there was chaos in the camp as women and bairns struggled to get into the safety of the wagons and men scrambled to muster what tools they had for weapons. There would be no searching for the lad now, not when these men needed to be herded into fighting stances.

"Don't huddle like sheep!" Conor shouted at them. "Spread out and watch from your points!"

He might as well be trying to command sheep, he decided, for they continued to bump and mill about, turning this way and that, eyes wide and white. The air fairly stank with their fear. So he pushed past them, heading towards the edge of the camp closest to the range of sounds. A battle was being fought in the forest. The snarls and snapping of jaws, the shriek when an animal was injured.

And then in the middle, a flash of light so bright, it burned patches of red across Conor's eyes and left him blinking.

At least he now knew where his son was. In the thick of whatever war was being fought. He took off loping towards the wood, painfully aware of the limit of his vision. He brushed through the circle of light and heard

Eithne call his name and a warning.

He barely turned in time as a shadow lunged at him. He saw the shape of a wolf, and eyes like firebrands, but there seemed to be no substance to the thing when he dove aside and lashed at it with his sword. It flew past, skidded in the sedge, and turned to rush at him again. Once more, he waited until the last moment and threw himself aside and cut the beast with his sword. He was certain he had taken off its head, yet he felt no resistance to his steel.

I'm fighting naught but a shadow! It was a grim thought that drove him to race back towards the circle. He needed to get inside the light, away from the dark creature's place of power. But it charged him again, and he threw himself down rather than be touched by its mist-like presence.

The paws that thumped the ground past him sounded heavy enough. Conor rolled onto his back and looked up to see a wolf with fire eyes staring at him. It growled and started to lunge once more.

"No!" Eithne screamed.

She came out of the ring of light like a fury, scooping up ensorcelled clumps of glowing grass and throwing them at the beast. One struck it and hit solid, and the beast gave a whimper and backed away.

It canna stand the light!

Eithne had clearly surmised this herself, and she seized up another clump of Rhoyd's magic light and tossed it over to where Conor lay. He seized it up, rubbing it down the blade of his sword, charging to his feet in one motion. Where the soil and grass touched his steel, a faint glow formed.

The shadow wolf turned for Conor and charged once more. He dodged again, and this time, his steel met solid form. The wolf screamed as his blade bit deep and drove light inside it. The creature turned to a puff of black smoke and vanished.

Down in the forest, Conor could hear only silence now.

He charged down the hill once more, heading towards the woods. Eithne followed, bringing two torches. He slowed down enough to take one of the torches from her and hurried on ahead.

Shadows closed over them as they stepped into the trees, but the fire cast amber about the wood. Conor surged towards the place where he knew the farmers had died. He could hear the rustle and whimpers and a murmuring feminine voice saying, "Brown Chaser will keep watch." Then the sounds seemed to scatter into the night.

He broke into the clearing and heard the growl of a wolf. Turning with his torch, he spotted a large brown one that bared teeth. Conor raised his sword, and the wolf held ground briefly before changing its mind. It issued one mournful howl, and then disappeared into the brush.

Rhoyd was seated on the ground, leaning over a wolf of lighter coloring. He tenderly ran his hands across the wolf's pelt. The creature's breathing was shallow and panting, and Conor could see blood spreading from the vicious wound in its side. Rhoyd's hands and tunic bore crimson stains as well, and the sight of that crimson swatch quelled Conor's anger under concern.

Beside the boy lay the spear, unsheathed, its blade glowing faintly, but there was no blood on the steel.

"Rhoyd?" Conor said, glancing at Eithne.

Rhoyd looked up. Tears tracked his cheeks, mingling with more blood. "She's dying," he whispered. "Eithne, can you help her?"

Eithne heaved a sigh and shook her head, carefully advancing as she set the end of her torch into the ground. Conor felt impelled to stand his ground, stand guard, as his wife knelt next to the boy.

"I'm sorry, Rhoyd," Eithne said. "My gift does not extend to animals, I fear."

"But it hurts," Rhoyd sobbed. "I feel her death and it hurts!"

"Did you do this?" Conor asked, gesturing towards the

wounded beast with his torch.

Rhoyd shook his head, flinging tears. "She tried to save me. She got between us when the Shadow Wolf attacked and..."

His words mumbled off to trembling sobs that shook him so hard, he could barely stay upright. Conor sighed and stepped carefully around behind Rhoyd. He cast one last cautious look at the forest, then knelt and laid his sword and the torch aside and put his hands on Rhoyd's shoulders to steady the lad.

The wolf ceased to breathe and relaxed against Rhoyd's thighs. "No," he whimpered.

Another mournful howl sounded, chorused by others so that the night once more belonged to the song of the wolves. Conor looked around in uncertainty.

What in the name of Cernunnos was happening?

Eithne became the voice of practicality. "Come on," she said as she moved around beside the lad and slipped arms under his. "Let's get you back to camp and get you cleaned up before all this blood sets in."

Conor stepped back and let her take charge. Rhoyd offered no resistance as Eithne coaxed him to his feet and started him out of the woods, snatching up her torch as she passed it. Conor collected the spear and studied the blade. There was a hint of some blackish residue--the Shadow Wolf? He frowned as he wiped it on the ground and sheathed the point with the wooden dragon, then picked up his sword and torch and followed.

He just hoped the lad would be more forthcoming about why he left camp late at night.

Eithne peeled Rhoyd out of his bloody clothes and washed his hands and face with a damp towel as they stood in the privacy of a wagon loaned them by one of the farmers. Around her dangled, rattled, and crammed into whatever space not needed to sleep was the paraphernalia of a simple life, tools, washboard, bundles of wool cloth.

The reek of lanolin was stronger here.

Rhoyd had yet to say a word. Now, he looked so small and pitiful that she wanted to draw him into her arms and just hold him. He stood there with his arms across his chest, his eyes half-closed, and offered no resistance to her ministering. At last, she deemed him clean enough to slip into his spare shirt and trews. The only clean tunic in his pack had been the brilliant blue one that his Aunt Genna made him wear when he took lessons from her. Eithne tried not to frown as he pulled it over his head, for it made it clear to all who saw him that he was mageborn.

"Better now?" she asked as she put the towel aside.

Rhoyd nodded and took a deep breath. He flinched when Conor barked an order to one of the farmers.

Yes, there is that, she thought. But she smiled and took his chin in hand, forcing his eyes to meet her gaze.

"Why were you there?" Eithne asked.

Rhoyd blinked. "I had to go. I promised," he said.

"Promised?" Eithne frowned. "Promised who? Promised what?"

He pulled back out of her grasp, and she did nothing to stop him as he walked over to the front of the wagon and peered out through a gap in the canvas.

"Conor is going to be so angry," he muttered.

Eithne sighed and followed him over. "Conor loves you, though it bothers him when you keep secrets," she said. "But then, you should know that by now."

"But I have to keep secrets, some things, at least," he said and sighed again. "Magic ones, according to Aunt Genna, are not to be shared."

"Was it magic that called you into the woods?"

"More like destiny," he said in such a serious tone, it sent a shiver right through her. "There is something I have to do."

"What?"

Rhoyd hesitated. "I have to tell Conor."

"You can tell Conor and not me?" Eithne asked.

Rhoyd glanced at her. His eyes brimmed with unshed

129

tears. "I have to tell him first."

Eithne nodded, putting her hands on his shoulders, and pressing lips gently to his cheek. "Then tell him," she said. "I can wait."

Rhoyd nodded, then pulled out from under her hands and crawled into the wagon seat. She watched as he hopped down and started across the camp to where Conor stood looking out at the dark with a wary warrior's eye.

The farmers were building bigger fires and huddling around them as Rhoyd crossed the camp. He stopped beside Conor, looking up at the tall red-haired Keltoran who stared at the woods.

"So, what was it this time?" Conor asked.

Rhoyd took a deep breath. This wasn't going to be easy.

"Fearfaolan," he said softly, not wanting the farmers to hear. "I went to meet them because I promised I would."

Conor's gaze rounded, narrowed in thought. His face otherwise was set in a hardened mask that made Rhoyd just a whit uneasy. Anger, frustration, and disappointment--all of them were visible in the expression. "You promised them? And what about your promises to me?"

Rhoyd bit his lip and shivered because his skin was still damp, and the wind was a bit cold. "Do you want to hit me?" he ventured.

Conor's fist tightened as though temptation existed, but he looked back out at the night. "I'm not a bully, lad," he said, "and you're getting too old to have yer trews dusted. Besides, a braw man like me hits a small lad like you... I'd just have to listen to the woman complaining about the bruises." He paused and looked back at Rhoyd. "But you've got to stop keeping secrets," Conor continued. "How can I trust your word if you keep secrets from me?"

"I'm sorry," Rhoyd said. "I had to do it."

"Why?"

"Because they said they would tell me."

"Tell you what?" Conor asked.

"What happened before and why I was dreaming about that monster." Rhoyd paused as his thoughts flowed. His dreams. He had not dreamed since before they reached Heatherbloom. "You know, I have not had a dream in several nights, not since I met them..."

Conor sighed and looked out at the woods. "So, they're real," he said in a controlled voice.

Rhoyd nodded, even though he knew Conor could not see him do so. "Yes. They're very real, and they're frightened because that creature is their worst enemy. And because it could bring back the Shadow Lord known as Dubh Sealgair."

"Horns," Conor muttered. "I have not heard that one mentioned since the Last War."

"You know of him?"

"All Keltorans know of him, lad," Conor said. "They say he ruled the southern lands in an age before the Great Cataclysm when shadows spread. He was the master of all Black Hunters."

"The beast in my dreams belongs to him. It was set free when Mistress Brina died, and now it seeks to destroy me and to free its master."

Conor's eyes narrowed.

"Is that what all this is about? The dreams, that spear, your nightly excursions?"

"They said I had to stop it," Rhoyd said.

Now Conor's eyebrows rose, and he turned and looked down at Rhoyd. "And what did you tell them."

Shrugging, Rhoyd took a deep breath. "I gave my word that I would try, but I'm not sure how I'm supposed to do it."

Conor's expression softened as he opened his arms. Rhoyd threw himself into the embrace, huddling close.

"I suppose you'll do what you know best to do," Conor said. "But ye'll not be doing it alone. I'll be with you."

"Thank you," Rhoyd said.

"No more secrets," Conor said.

"No more secrets," Rhoyd repeated and drew back a little. "So, I guess I should tell you about the wolf?"

Conor frowned. "What wolf?"

"His name's Brown Chaser, and he's been told to follow me and look after me until we reach the Faolanwold."

He watched as Conor's mouth twitched sideways.

"All right," he finally said. "But know this. I don't clean up after wolves…"

Rhoyd grimaced. He hoped it didn't come to that.

NINE

Come morning, they parted ways with the farmers. Conor assured them that Coldforge was close enough to reach before the next nightfall, and then he and his family set their course towards the peaks of Ben Faolan. The mountain was little more than a blue misty silhouette just now, but Conor knew that in another couple of days, it would grow as dark and ominous as the thoughts in his heart.

How in the name of Cernunnos are we going to stop a monster? Granted, he had seen so much magic since the Last War, more so now that Rhoyd was part of their lives. Conor could not help worrying about the lad. Rhoyd was growing--very slowly--and while his confidence with magic remained high, Conor worried that the lad's spirit was not so keen on the tasks that fate had chosen for him. *By all the gods, he has more growing to do before he can be a' saving the world. It's too soon. He's just a lad...*

A lad with the power to burn demons and call fire. A lad who carried a bit of demon bone in a pouch around his neck. A lad who had nearly been taken away by one Conor once called friend...

Maybe I am the one who is not ready for this. The thought of losing Rhoyd did not set well in Conor's gut. He knew the lad had to grow up and fulfill the destiny his uncle's spirit was always hinting at when his Auntie was not around to hear. His uncle--how about every man, woman and child in this miserable world? The more they see of what he can do, the more they come to depend on him. It was one of the reasons Conor wanted "the glamorie" to stay out of their lives as much as possible.

He did not begrudge the lad his skill and fate, but in a world where men either worshiped those born to power or considered them as evil as the demons the lad had slain, he knew too well the risks.

They would slaughter him--or take him from me, and by the Horns, I'll not see that happen.

It was selfish, he realized, but he refused to see it any other way.

Their trail was growing winding and narrow again, taking them through braes and glens and forests. Now and again, evidence of farmsteads faced them, places where the land had been cleared and crops sown. But he saw too the evidence of destruction the beast was leaving.

They found a farmstead, mostly in ruins, and boarded themselves into it for the night. Conor kept vigil. Now and again, he would hear an animal breathing, and its panting would alert him. But Rhoyd would wake up long enough to mumble something about this Brown Chaser, and then slide back into a peaceful sleep.

Well, at least he's not having those horrid dreams.

Which led him to wonder why the lad believed his dreams would only stop once this "beast" was put back in its prison.

The hours of night passed slowly. Conor nodded off and drifted into dreams where everyone around him had the head of some beast. They crowded him, forcing him to follow a path through a cavern until he stood on a precipice. Below was a river as red as blood that rushed swiftly past him and spilled into a winding ravine. Where it led, he did not know, but the creatures were pushing him towards it, encouraging him to jump.

Be not afraid, man of steel and words. Let the power take you where it chooses, for your destiny will lie at the end.

And with that, one of the creatures rushed at Conor and caught him around the middle, shoving him over the edge. He fell, clutching the creature only to find it was not a creature at all but Rhoyd who looked up from under black hair, blue eyes shining.

Be not afraid...

They hit the water as one, yanked into the dark depths and then spat out again as the river dragged them onward.

"Don't let go," Rhoyd said. "Please, Conor, don't let go!"

But some force seemed to be dragging at Conor, fingers of darkness, wrapping around him, folding over him like a wave and pulling him down. He let go, fearful that he would drag the lad to this watery doom.

Rhoyd would not let go.

Conor tried to shake him off, and with a shout that filled his lungs with water, he pushed the lad away and watched Rhoyd swept towards the surface while he sank like a stone, clawing for a simple breath of air that would never come.

With a gasp, Conor opened his eyes and sat up.

The world around him was pale with dawn's light. Rhoyd and Eithne were over by the fire, looking at him with uncertainty filling their eyes. The woman was molding bannocks with her hands.

"Are you all right?" she asked.

Conor sighed and nodded. "Just dreaming," he said.

Rhoyd's eyes narrowed in thought. Conor avoided the glance and crawled to his feet to stretch the stiff kinks out of his muscles.

Nothing felt right to Eithne that day. She watched as Conor rode to the front, his eyes straying over the world like a man expecting a monster to leap out at him from every tree and hummock and stone. Rhoyd seemed less stressed than he had in a while. He was sleeping again, which she deemed a blessing, but now she worried that Conor was not sleeping. His eyes had grown even more hollow.

Before they left that musty old farmstead this morning, he had pulled Rhoyd aside and spoken to the lad out of her hearing range. When the conversation ended, Conor looked darkly unhappy and Rhoyd a bit sad.

"So 'twill be no avoiding it?" Conor asked when they came back inside where she had finished packing the bedrolls.

Rhoyd had shaken his head.

"Avoid what?" she had asked.

"Nothing," Conor said and turned away from her to work on loading his own pack.

"You asked if there would be no avoiding it," Eithne firmly insisted. "I want to know what we have to face that we would rather avoid."

"Just the road, woman," Conor said in a surly tone. "We might run into a storm so we're going to have to take a different trail."

"A storm?" She had glanced at Rhoyd then, and the lad would not meet her gaze.

"Give it a rest, woman," Conor said. "We've been wet before. Now let's get on the road as quick as we can."

He put his back to her after that, refusing to even look at her as they saddled and loaded the horses, and then mounted up for the ride.

The whole conversation had left her with a worm of discontent wriggling in her stomach. She rode in silence, wishing there were more cheerful sounds.

They took a turn entering a forest of pines before the middle of the day. The tangy scent of conifer needles hung heavy in the air. Normally, such an odor would have comforted her, but now, her nerves stood on edge. She didn't remember them going this way before. She sighed and glanced at Rhoyd who was riding beside her. Until now, his nose had been buried in a book, but as they slipped into the shade of the trees, he looked up and frowned. She followed the direction of his gaze. Something flitted the length of a branch and disappeared behind the trunk. Eithne raised an eyebrow. Was that a black squirrel? She had never seen one that color before.

She shook the dread aside. *I am being ridiculous,* she thought and glanced once more at Rhoyd who had returned to reading. A slight tension stiffened his shoulders.

"Is that a good book?" she asked him when he paused from his perusal of the pages.

Rhoyd cast a startled look at her. "Yes," he said warily.

"What's it about?" she asked.

"It's a journal," he said, as though uncertain he should be telling her such things. "Kept by my great uncle Fenelon."

"Really. I bet he had some fascinating things to write about."

"I guess," Rhoyd said and folded the book shut after marking his page with the strip of leather that dangled from the top of the book's leather cover.

"You guess?" she repeated and glanced once more at their surroundings. The air was considerably cooler here, and a damp odor now mixed with the pine. "You seem quite absorbed by it. What was he writing about?"

A sheen of panic entered his expression. "Well, he just talks about old spells and such that he learned from the Demon-Bound."

"Such as?"

Rhoyd hesitated again. "Well, like using the walking stones."

"Walking stones?" Eithne frowned. "Stones that actually walk?"

Rhoyd shook his head and grinned. "No, they're gateways to other places. And if one knows the spell, one can open them and step through into other lands."

"Well, that sounds quite fascinating to me," Eithne said, and offered a reassuring smile. "I would think it would be a wondrous thing to be able to step into a stone and be someplace else. Think of all the time caravans could save if they could walk through a stone and be at the end of their journey."

Rhoyd relaxed and his smile widened. "They were used

just that way at one time according to what Fenelon says," he said. "But apparently when the Shadow Lords came into power, they abused the walking stones, so the Old Ones destroyed some of them, and people who thought magic was evil broke others. The few stones remaining are hidden. According to Fenelon, the Demon-Bound taught him the spells, but refused to share the location of those that led to the Center of All Things with him."

"Ah," Eithne said and shook her head. "How sad."

She glanced up into the trees again, and this time was struck by the odd silence that filled the air. And through the dark shadows of the green, she swore she saw a stand of tall menhirs. Indeed, they looked like the legs of some giant beast, and when she followed them, they rose over her like an archway. *What is this place?* She glanced down at the road. There were broken cobbles scattered about. And rows of low walls of stone.

"Just where are we?" she asked.

Rhoyd glanced around. His gaze turned serious. "I think it's a gate," he said.

"Like the walking stones?" she asked, arching her eyebrows.

"You don't really care about the walking stones," Rhoyd said.

"No, I suppose not," she said and leaned towards him. "I just wanted to hear a voice besides the one running around in my head. And I am a bit worried about Conor. I mean, what did the two of you talk about this morning?"

Rhoyd's eyes went wide. "Uh..."

"No whispering behind me back, woman," Conor suddenly said and half turned in the saddle so he could look back at her. "Especially when ye mention me name."

"Only with the greatest of affection," she replied, looking sharply at him.

"I bet ye say that to all the mercenaries," Conor said with a sneer.

"No, just to the one I love."

He smiled and glanced forward again, and to her delight, he started to sing.

"There's a wind blawing o're the meadow
As sweet as the breath of new spring
It brings me the scent of the heather
And tells me I'm homeward bound.

I can smell the peat fire a' burning.
I can smell the wet flow of the burn
I can smell that the bannocks need turning
And ken I be homeward bound..."

Eithne smiled at the thought. Well, maybe things were not as bad as they seemed.

At least she did until she saw the shadows creeping through the trees. Memories of darklings and demons assailed her. Of the time the darkling rushed at her and Rhoyd across a moonlit moor. And of the shadow wolves that had attacked the farmer's caravan just a few nights back. *They've been following us!* She opened her mouth, pointed, and shouted, "There!"

Conor turned in the saddle, ripping his sword free of the scabbard. Rhoyd turned as well. The shadow was rushing towards him blindingly fast. He raised his hand and shouted "Solus!"

Eithne blinked at the bright light that suddenly assailed her eyes. The thing in the shadows screamed and fled. Rhoyd threw the light after the beast, and Eithne watched as it rolled into the trees, watched as several shadows fled like living things.

Another shadow rose behind them and snarled. And in the trees, smaller ones started to creep out onto the branches.

Darkness began to swell, like a cloud pulling over the face of the sun. The wind picked up and whipped leaves into a whorl across the road ahead and behind.

"Blessed Brother," she cried.

Conor suddenly joined them, staring in awe at the whorls that were drawing closer and closer. "Let's get out of these woods now," he said.

"Which way?" Eithne asked. There seemed to be no way visible now. And with the growing dark, tiny forms gathered in the branches, things with bright red eyes.

"This way!" Rhoyd said and spurred Moonface up into the trees. "Follow us!"

Us? Who was the lad talking about?

"Just do as the lad says," Conor said as he shifted around so he was taking up the rear. Eithne, her hands shaking so hard she could barely hold the reins, pressed heels into Maudie's side and urged the stubborn little mare on. They rode fast and hard, dodging through the trees and the shrubs, eager to get out of the small forest that now appeared to be crawling with shadow creatures. And up ahead of the lad, some shape was fleeing. She glanced back at the whorl. The two circles had met and become one, and now they were spreading out to overtake the rest of the wood.

Her heart in her chest, Eithne looked forward again, when something the size of a squirrel leapt out of one of the trees and landed on Maudie's neck. The mare panicked and plunged forward. The creature looked like some sort of black rat, except it could not hold its form. Red eyes narrowed and it chattered--or was it some sort of maniacal laugh? It lunged towards Eithne, and she screamed and slapped at it as hard as she could. Her hand hit something rather like a wet sponge, and the creature flumped off the mare's neck and hit the ground.

Conor was shouting to keep going. The whorl was now filling the air over their heads, reminding her of the death wind they once encountered. Leaves and detritus were kicked up so that Eithne could not be certain which way she went. She barely made out the boy ahead of her, shouting for them to follow him. Conor disappeared behind her. She felt panic surging through her, but she kept urging the mare on, following Rhoyd's voice.

Then suddenly, she passed through the whorl, and out of the trees. Ahead of her she could see Rhoyd. He turned Moonface around and shouted, "Solus!" again. This time, his white light spread like a wave, crashing through the woods, and turning the shadows away, slamming into the edges of the whorl. Screaming filled the air, the death squeals of the tiny black beasts, the meeting of magic. Eithne thought her own voice might have been added to the fray as she rode past the boy.

She managed to drag Maudie to a halt, though where she found the strength, she could not say. Pulling the mare around so she and Eithne faced the woods again, Eithne stared at the trees.

Conor! Blessed Brother, where is Conor?

She was about to press heels into the mare and go riding back when Conor came riding out with several small dark forms clinging to his saddle and his armor and Battlebrute's mane. Two larger ones shaped like wolves were on Battlebrute's heels, their jaws snapping close to the warhorse's hamstrings. The smaller beasts were growling and gnawing at him and his warhorse like ravenous rats. But as soon as Rhoyd's wall of light hit them, they screamed and turned into puffs of black smoke. Conor pulled Battlebrute to a halt just beside the pair, coughing and hacking at the offensive odor now hanging around him in the dissipating black mist.

"What were those things?" Eithne asked.

"I don't know," Conor said, then cleared his throat and spat. "We'll be staying out of the woods even if it means leaving the road." He glanced at Rhoyd. "Are ye all right, lad? Did the spell work?"

Rhoyd's face was white.

"Spell? Rhoyd?" Eithne said. "What is the matter?"

Rhoyd shook his head. "I'm fine," he said.

"Then why do you look so..."

Eithne stopped. Conor was looking at something beyond her gaze. She turned around.

A mountain rose, black as death, its summit disappearing into the clouds.

"Where are we?" she asked?

"In the Faolanwold near Ben Faolan," Conor said.

"But this isn't the road we've taken before," she insisted. "We're still a few days away."

"Nay, it is not," Conor agreed. "But they said it was the only way."

"Only way to what?" Eithne demanded as she glanced back at the woods. The trees even looked different. They had been in a forest of pines before, but what she saw now was a grove of ancient oaks, and poked through the tops, tall pinnacles of stone meeting at the center to form an arch.

"Walking stones," Rhoyd said and pointed. "They brought us here. It was one of the spells I was studying in Fenelon's journal. They said I needed to learn the spell to get us here faster because the shadow wolves were still on our trail."

"Who told you this?" Eithne insisted.

Before Rhoyd could answer her, a shape moved out from behind him. A wolf with something hooded on its back. Eithne pointed and started to scream a warning to the lad, But Rhoyd shook his head.

"There's nothing to fear," he said. "That's Brown Chaser and Greymoon. They're the ones who led us through the walking stone gate."

The small being shook the remains of leaves and dust from their hood, and then pushed back the edge of her cloak. Eithne gasped as the face of a beast peered up at her from the hood's depths.

"Welcome to the Faolanwold, mother of the Ard Magister," the creature said.

Eithne slipped off Maudie's back, clinging to the saddle before her legs turned to liquid and she sank to the ground in a shaking puddle.

"Who in the name of the Blessed Brother are you?" she

asked.

The creature dismounted and approached, squatting before Eithne. Musk filled the air. Vixen features stretched with a grin.

"I am Fearfaolan," she said. "And I am here to help your son."

TEN

"And just when were you planning to tell me about all this?" Eithne asked.

Rhoyd winced as he sat off to one side on a stone and watched Conor and Eithne from a short distance. Brown Chaser lay at his feet like a hearth dog, ever vigilant to the stones of the mountain rising to their east. Greymoon squatted beside the wolf, tracing the ground with the end of her staff.

"I didn't see it as anything you needed to concern ye, woman," Conor replied. "We're safe for now."

"Really, and how can you think this would not concern me? After all, if the pair of you go marching off into the mountains without me to do battle with some dark power, what am I supposed to think if you do not return?"

Conor clamped his mouth in a line.

"It is good to know she cares," Greymoon said softly. "But she cannot come to the mountain with us."

Rhoyd glanced at the Fearfaolan and frowned. "What do you mean?"

"Her mother instincts will interfere in what you must do." Greymoon reached over and scratched Brownchaser's ears. "She will distract you and the man, and endanger us all. She must stay behind, or all will be lost."

Rhoyd turned his gaze back to the arguing pair. Eithne's hands were on her hips in a gesture of defiance. Conor bristled like an old boar over the challenge.

"But where can she stay?" Rhoyd asked.

"There is a cavern not far from here where some of my

kin still dwell," Greymoon said. "We will go there first. The clan will look after her while you and I and the man ascend the mountain."

"Why are you coming?"

"I am your guide, remember," Greymoon said with a lupine smile. "I was there in your dream."

Rhoyd frowned at the Fearfaolan. "If you were the one in my dream, why did you chide me for challenging the dark?" he said.

"Aye, well" she said. "When you provoked the Venomous Dark and broke the bones of the Elderkin, you set in motion a pattern of events. Do you still have a bit of bone?"

Rhoyd reached up and touched the small sack he wore about his neck now--the only way he knew to keep the bone from touching the ground.

"The Venomous Dark was defeated," Rhoyd said. "I drove him back into the ground."

"Aye, and your brave act assured us all he will not rise again for a time, at least not until the next Darkening sets him free," she said.

"Then why should I worry?"

"There is a Balance that must be maintained," Greymoon said wearily. "You broke the bones of the Elderkin. Now the Balance is threatened, and you must be ready to deal with the consequences. You know what that means, do you not?"

Rhoyd fought the urge to roll his eyes. He had been hearing about this Balance for a couple of years now. "There is no shadow without light, no day without night," he said. "So?"

"You drove the shadow into the depths, but you also gave the shadow a weapon."

"What?" Rhoyd asked. "What weapon?"

"Unfortunately, another fragment of the bone of the Elderkin was left behind," she said. "Our enemies will use that when the time of the Darkening is at hand."

146

"How was I to know?" Rhoyd said. "I mean, how is it you know?"

"Each time you do something that makes the Balance of All Things shift even in the minutest of fashion, it sends a ripple through the world that all who are attuned to such things know. But you should know this. The one who trains you should be teaching you this. You should feel it as well."

"My Aunt Genna trains me, and according to my Uncle Fenelon's spirit, she is withholding spells I need to know now, which is why he lets me take his journals and not tell her that I have them. But no one ever tells me what I really need to know, so how can I possibly know what I am supposed to know and..."

Greymoon made a clucking sound and waved him off, for Conor was stalking across the ground with Eithne at his side. Neither of them looked very happy. Rhoyd grimaced, wondering if he might have been better off slipping away without telling Conor or Eithne now.

"We need to find shelter," Conor said.

"There is shelter of a sort," Greymoon said, looking up at Conor's great height. "My kin have a cavern close by. We can find safety and shelter there."

Conor arched an eyebrow. "Will we have to sleep with wolves?" he asked.

"Does that trouble you?" she returned.

Conor shrugged. "I've slept with worse, I imagine," he said and turned to Eithne. "Assuming the woman agrees."

Eithne shot him a look that would have burned had it been a firebrand. She crossed her arms and met Greymoon's steady gaze.

"There are probably those among my kin who will welcome a True Healer such as yourself," Greymoon said. "For often there are illnesses and wounds to be treated."

"I can try, but I am not really sure my skills work on animals," Eithne said, but then her face colored even as those words slipped out of her mouth.

Greymoon merely smiled. "I doubt our wolves will have

needs," she said. "But I can assure you, that we Fearfaolan are not animals, though we may appear to be beast to your innocent eyes. But you should know this, having assisted the birth of one of our half kin."

"I am sorry, I meant no offense," Eithne said warily.

"None is taken," Greymoon said with a nod. "But as you can see, this face is the reason we must hide from others."

Eithne bowed her head and nodded. "Then I will gladly accept your hospitality," she said. "And do what I can for those who have need."

"Good," Conor said. "I'll get the horses. How far?"

"Perhaps half a league," Greymoon said.

He hurried off to recapture their grazing mounts. Eithne hesitated then followed him down the slope.

Rhoyd looked at Greymoon. "How will you keep her there?" he asked.

"Trust me, there is need among my kin that her skills can work on, and she will be too occupied to see us leave."

Rhoyd sighed. He hoped she was right.

He knew better than to upset Eithne. Quiet though she might be, even Conor walked on eggs when she was in a temper.

They rode eastward with Greymoon astride Brown Chaser as though the wolf was a horse. Conor could not help but notice that the world seemed a bit grey and gloomy for the time of day. The moor they crossed was rugged and rocky, the sort that would lame a horse if a man were not careful, but the Fearfaolan took them on the surest path among the stones and the stunted trees that added their gnarled shape to the rough landscape.

He had not seen a land so desolate since the Last War. There were places in upper Tamnagh and lower Elenthorn just like this. The Hound left his mark on everything when he tried to conquer the Fourteen Kingdoms of Ard-Taebh, and the scars of his passing were not so easily forgotten in the north. And yet, as Conor rode past stones that vaguely held the shapes of men--stones he was certain he had never seen before--he felt something ancient, a wicked malaise that he did not associate with any other part of Keltora he had ever passed through in his life.

But this is not the way we passed before, he thought. *Our road lies to the north of the Faolanwold.* Had this place been this way for so long? Or was it the result of the malaise released only a moon ago.

Their path took an upward rise. Greymoon dismounted from her wolf and glanced back at Conor. "We shall have to walk from here," she said. "The path is too steep for the horses to carry you safely."

Conor nodded and dismounted. Eithne looked a little put out to have to let go of the comfort of her saddle on such terrain. Rhoyd hopped down without question.

They started on up the trail. It wound back and forth through the stones, always ascending the lower mountain face. As a result, the trek took much longer. To Conor's mind they had gone no more than a tenth of a league when Greymoon stopped and raised her hand.

"Wait here," she said.

He stopped, holding Battlebrute's reins. The old warhorse shoved Conor's shoulder for attention or sheer contrariness--Conor could never be certain--forcing him to grab the noseband of the bridle to keep the horse from getting rougher.

Greymoon clambered up on top of one of the ill-shaped outcrops of stone. She took a deep breath and raised her head. A keen escaped her lips, not unlike the yipping howl of a fox.

It was answered tenfold.

"I am Greymoon of the Heatherbloom Clan. I come in peace, and I bring guests as well. Will you allow us the hospitality of your cavern?"

Suddenly there was movement all over the mountainside. More than one diminutive shape stirred from the shadows and outcrops of rock and the depths of sedge and heather. A pack sprang into view, some crouching on all fours, some standing upright. Conor saw weapons, small swords, daggers, cudgels and short quarterstaffs. Unlike Greymoon, these warriors were barely dressed in kilts of wool whose tartan patterns were hardly discernible. Some of them even had the fur of their faces and the smoother skin of their bodies painted in woad. They looked more like savage animals. Or highland bandits.

He slipped his hand to the hilt of his sword.

One of the smaller dark-furred males started to charge, but a female of larger size suddenly stepped into his path and snapped at him. He bared teeth as he backed down. She turned back to them, her vixen face covered in pale gold fur. With one yellow eye fixed on Conor as though to warn him, she stepped forward and stopped just before Greymoon.

"Why are you here, old mother?" the younger Fearfaolan asked.

"I see you have not forgotten me, Goldmane" Greymoon said.

"How can we forget the one who banished her own daughter from the Heatherbloom Clan and forced her to live in this place," Goldmane said, and she spat on the ground.

"We all do our part to preserve the Balance of All Things," Greymoon said. "And you were given the choice. I could have just as easily sent another of my pups to lead the clan here."

"You have come at a bad time," Goldmane said. "The shadows have spat forth the Cu' Deamhan. To stand here is to risk its wrath."

"I have brought one to put the demon back in its crypt," Greymoon said. She leaned forward. "I have brought the Chosen One."

Goldmane glanced around Greymoon at Conor. "He is too old to be the Chosen One," she said.

"He is the father, and that is the mother, and there is the one who will one day set the Balance aright."

"Or spin it off center as some of the elders have said," Goldmane said and snorted. "Come, you are all welcome here. The shadows will soon prowl the night, so it is best we get into the caverns and set the fire watches."

Goldmane turned and barked commands to her clan. The Fearfaolan pack slowly disappeared.

"This way," Goldmane said.

Greymoon leapt off the rocks to follow. Conor looked uncertain at first, but he glanced at the shadows around them.

They were growing thicker as the sun canted itself westward.

He followed, dragging his warhorse up the steep path.

At length, it opened out into a level area. Several Fearfaolan stood watch now. They only glanced at him and his family, showing no fear, and then turned their eyes back out to the world as though unconcerned.

"The horses can go in here," Goldmane said. "There is a place that we keep livestock."

Conor was grateful that the opening was tall enough for him to pass under without ducking his head. He stepped into a gloomy cave, his eyes straining to adjust to the lack of light. But then he heard Rhoyd whisper, *"Solus,"* and felt the tickle of magic. Light flooded the way.

"Druidh," was whispered through the cave and echoed in the distance as the word was repeated by various tongues. Conor frowned, uncertain what it meant.

Goldmane stopped them and gestured to a side passage. Conor smelled the odor of cattle and sheep. He led Battlebrute into a chamber where lanterns glowed. Here the rock had been cut even, and stalls of wood with bedding of straw had been built. By Fearfaolan hand? He did not think they had such skills. They lived in caves like animals.

"You may leave your horses there for the night. They will be safe."

Conor put Battlebrute into one of the stalls. Eithne and Rhoyd followed suit. They pulled packs from the animals as Goldmane and Greymoon waited. Once all was set, the Fearfaolan led them out of the stabling cave and into a long narrow passage. Here, there was an unnatural glow on the walls. Conor stepped over to one side to examine it and felt magic.

Greymoon was suddenly at his side. Her eyes studied his expression. She reached out with a hand and touched the cavern walls.

"Fascinating, is it not?" she asked.

"Aye," Conor said.

"These caverns once served as the entrance to a great underground city built by Stone Folk, some say," Greymoon said. "The deepest passages have long ago collapsed, but this part is safe."

Conor nodded and moved on with the others. He had already seen Rhoyd turning around and looking at everything he could, even the ceiling. Conor glanced overhead and noticed that the stonework here looked like old archways, and there were carvings of all manner of natural and unnatural beasts.

The lad dashed forward to catch up with Conor.

The passage led to a larger chamber and there the odors of musk, pelts, and other animal scents he associated with their dens in the wild, mingled with the aroma of roasting hens and bannocks.

"They make bannocks?" Conor said. Despite the canine stench filling the air, his mouth watered at the thought.

"We are not so different in our likes and dislikes," Greymoon said. "Bannocks fill the belly well."

He stopped and looked around. It reminded him of some of the refugee camps he had seen during the Last War, when folks from the north fled south seeking to stay ahead of the Haxon hordes. But here, every face that peered at him and his small family was that of a fox, though to his surprise, he saw differences as well. Some were foxier than others. Some reminded him more of wolves, and at least one chubby fellow looked more like an old Keltoran staghound.

"We have guests," Goldmane said. "They come in peace, and we will treat them as our own."

Some looks were traded. Others went about their business as though strangers were not so uncommon. Conor saw all the same activities he would have expected in a human village.

Goldmane took them over to a place where there was room to settle packs. "If you must use fire, then use magic fire," she said. "I will have food brought to you."

"I sense need," Eithne said, looking astounded. "Who is ill?"

Goldmane's brows arched. "You are a True Healer, then?"

"Yes," Eithne said.

"This is good," Goldmane said. "Several of our women are about to whelp, and we have injured warriors as well."

"Then take me to them," Eithne said, gathering her healer kit.

"Do you want us to go with ye, woman?" Conor asked.

Eithne shook her head and followed Goldmane across the way. Though he noticed she reached into her pouch and rolled a bit of mint leaf under her nose.

"Good," Greymoon said. "You will eat and then we will leave. She should be quite busy for a time."

"But it's getting dark," Conor said.

"The dark is the time," Greymoon said. "The moon will rise and offer us light, but the time draws close. If we are not swift, the Shadow Lord will be set free before the next moon wanes."

Conor glanced at Rhoyd. The lad was nervously fiddling with the dragonhead of his staff.

Yer not eager for this, are ye lad, Conor thought. But I'll be there fae ye, have no fear.

He would do whatever he had to in order to keep his

adopted son alive tonight.

Rhoyd laughed aloud as a pair of Fearfaolan children tumbled and rolled about in a wrestling match. One would nip, one would yelp, one would curse in a very human tongue, and then they would be at one another again, snarling and snapping like small wolf pups. Others of their ilk sat around, encouraging the match with yips and cheers.

Beside him sat Brown Chaser as though it was his natural place. Rhoyd leaned over the wolf, feeling almost as comforted and protected as he did in Conor's arms. Now and again, Brown Chaser would reach around and lap Rhoyd's face, adding to his hilarity.

He was almost ready to believe that nothing else could possibly be wrong when he spied Greymoon at the mouth of the section of cavern where the youth of the Fearfaolan played with such wild abandon. Several of the younger ones by the entrance began to slink away from her as she entered the area at a steady pace. She was no longer wearing the robes that had adorned her small body on their trip here. Instead, she had decked herself out in leather armor, revealing the muscular womanly figure that so belied her vixen head. Brown Chaser thumped his tail at the sight of her.

She stopped at Rhoyd's side.

"It is time to leave," she said. "We want to be there before the moon is high."

"Where's Conor?" Rhoyd asked.

"He waits at the entrance," she said.

Reluctantly, Rhoyd crawled to his feet. Brown Chaser clambered up on all fours and trotted towards the mouth of the cavern as though nothing was amiss. With a deep breath, Rhoyd followed the wolf. The eyes of the Fearfaolan pups now followed him filled with a mixture of admiration and sorrow. He tried not to meet any of their gazes as he crawled after the wolf and headed for the main cavern with Greymoon on his heels.

Conor was indeed standing by the entrance, staring out at the darkness. He had several bundles at hand, and when Rhoyd stumbled over a loose pebble, the Keltoran turned.

"Here," Conor said. "Put this on."

He held out one of the bundles. Rhoyd unwrapped it to find a lightweight mail shirt.

"I was saving it for yer next birthday," he said. "I think ye'll be needing it tonight."

Rhoyd hesitated. Mail armor? He looked up at Conor and saw the hint of worry in the Keltoran's eyes. Taking a deep breath, Rhoyd unfurled the mail shirt. It was a little larger than he.

"I figured ye would grow into to," Conor said and the corner of his mouth twitched in amusement. "Come on, let's get it on ye."

Rhoyd nodded as Conor took the mail shirt and assisted the lad into it. The weight of it felt alien on his small shoulders. He had never worn armor before and wasn't sure if he liked it. Conor produced an old belt to cinch it in at Rhoyd's waist so it would not bang against his knees.

"Aye, ye do need to be a bit taller," Conor mused.

Rhoyd smiled to hide the sense that he didn't want to. Once he was armored, Conor held out the dragon headed spear.

"Two things," Conor said. "I know that Eithne has been working with ye on her quarterstaff, and this is no different, except that it's got a wicked bit of steel on one end. Just make sure ye keep yer hands about the span of yer own hips apart. That way, ye can maneuver it and control it."

"And the other thing?" Rhoyd asked.

"If all else fails, use yer magic to save yersel', aye?" Conor said.

Rhoyd nodded.

"Even if it means leaving the rest of us behind," Conor

added.

Rhoyd gasped and opened his mouth to protest, but a large finger crossed his lips.

"Promise me," Conor said. "Promise me if all else fails, you will save yourself and not give a thought to me. I won't have you risking your life for mine, even if I have vowed to risk mine for yours. But I'm not this Champion they keep talking about that will save the world one day. You save yourself if all else fails and do me proud."

Rhoyd bit his lip and blinked. He took a deep unsteady breath and nodded. "I promise," he whispered, though the very words burned his tongue.

"Good lad," Conor said and shuffled a hand through Rhoyd's hair. "Now let's go kill us a monster."

Greymoon had already started for the mouth of the cavern. Conor turned and followed her, and Rhoyd had no choice but to trail after them, especially since Brown Chaser butted his head into the small of Rhoyd's back to urge him on.

The path was not so easy, and it was steep, and the weight of the chain mail was pulling Rhoyd down. He slipped several times, and finally Brown Chaser nosed him and then lowered himself on his belly and whined. As Rhoyd looked up at the mountain, he saw Conor watching with a dubious stare. Silently, Rhoyd clambered aboard the wolf's back, pulling the staff under his arm to keep from banging it on shrubs and stones and trees.

"Ye look like yer about to enter the lists, lad," Conor said and grinned. "But I think yer steeds a bit short for the tournament."

Rhoyd sighed, grateful for the shadows that hid his embarrassment.

Greymoon smiled from beyond the Keltoran.

"Good, now we can make better time," she said and turned back to climbing the mountain's narrow trail.

Rhoyd rolled his eyes. This was not, he imagined, how

"champions" were supposed to travel. On the other hand, he felt grateful for the wolf's cooperation as well as his sure-footedness on the trail. And they did make better time, climbing the steep way until Greymoon motioned for them all to stand still. Rhoyd looked up and bit back the desire to express his wonder. Before them on the trail rose a set of old stones, most of which looked to have been knocked out of place by some great blow. Even from here, the moonlight revealed what looked like giant claw marks in the stone. And beyond that, barely visible through a hint of mist, stood several stones in all manner of sizes and shapes.

What happened here?

Past those shapes stood a forest of bare trees where shadows shifted and stirred, and through those blackened trunks, a path wandered in no straight line. Rhoyd stared, wondering just how it was he could see all this? It was as if he had been here before.

My dream! I saw this place in my dream.

The thought sent a shiver through him. The nightmare where he fled the beast had taken him over a moor, and through woods just like those. But he didn't remember running down a mountain. He glanced back at the moor below. There were jagged stones and corpses of boulders among the heather and sedge that littered the area below.

I was down there when it took me, he thought.

"We are at the first gate," Greymoon whispered and sniffed. "The beast's scent is here."

Conor drew his sword and his long dirk. He turned towards Rhoyd. "Put yer light on my steel, lad," he said, keeping his voice low. "Like ye did around the camp when the shadow wolves attacked."

"It may not be wise," Greymoon said. "The Cu' Deamhan will sense his magic, just as its master will. And the glow of your steel will be as beacons to our enemies' eyes. Do you want them to see us before we reach the top?"

We're not near the top? Rhoyd thought glumly as he

tried to see how far they still had to go.

"It's a chance I'll take if it gives me an edge," Conor said, and held his sword and long dagger out towards Rhoyd.

Rhoyd closed his eyes and reached for essence. He found it in the moonlight and air. Whispering mage words, he drew it to him, leaving just a hint of his concentration free. "Loisg feith," he said and touched his fingers to Conor's blade. Essence shimmered and shifted from his fingers, crawling the length of the sword. It took on the glow of white flames. He looked up as Conor stared at his blade and saw something reflected in the Keltoran's eyes--a sense of wonder that made Rhoyd smile.

But then Conor shivered as though a chill had passed down his spine and quickly thrust the glowing long dagger deep into his scabbard, keeping only a few inches free. The sword stayed in his hand, and he tossed the long end of his plaidie over it to hide the glow.

"Satisfied?" he asked.

Greymoon rolled her eyes, but she nodded all the same.

"All right," he said, looking at Greymoon. "Let's get this over with before the woman decides to follow us."

Greymoon shook her head and sighed. She motioned for them to hold back while she crept up to the stones, still sniffing the air. Rhoyd could taste the pungent scent in the air, and he could feel the malaise that darkened the earth as well. The shadows beyond the broken gate moved as though alive, ebbing like fog on a tide.

Greymoon was abreast of the main stones before she motioned that the way was clear. Conor hurried forward, and Brown Chaser loped up the short distance as though fresh as morning.

They passed under the stones and crossed the uneven path to enter the woods. Rhoyd was glancing around when Brown Chaser stopped and lowered himself to the ground, nearly toppling Rhoyd. He yelped with surprise.

Two pairs of eyes glared, and two voices hissed "Wheesht!"

"It wasn't my fault!" he protested quietly as he scrambled to get off the wolf without banging every tree in his reach with the staff. Briefly, he staggered then righted himself.

They shushed him again. He started to protest when he took a step to one side and felt cold.

Horns, it's a void! With a yelp, Rhoyd backed into the nearest tree and hit it with his staff. The wood clattered and Conor turned to admonish Rhoyd when Greymoon raised a hand.

"We are not alone," the Fearfaolan whispered and gestured about her.

Brown Chaser's hackles rose, and the wolf growled softly. Rhoyd looked out at the woods.

Shadows were moving in the shape of things that might have been wolves. But the familiar burn like cloves on his tongue told him what they really were.

Shadow demons. Shadow wolves!

"Now I think we need your white light," Greymoon said.

But before Rhoyd could move out of the void and hiss *"Solus!"* one of the shadows lunged out of the forest and rushed straight at Conor.

ELEVEN

Conor saw the creature as it slipped out of the shadows among the trees and took the form of a wolf. With a shout, he lashed out with his sword and felt the steel make solid contact with the intangible form. The shadow wolf yelped as his sword ripped open its chest, and it fell to the ground only to dissolve into smoke at his feet.

Its death cry did not go unanswered. A furious howl set up around them, filling the forest and echoing off the mountains. At once, every shadow came alive rushing out of the trees.

Rhoyd shouted *"Solus mhor!"* and the brilliance of his white light washed outward. Conor felt the magic pass, like heat on his skin, and yet it did not burn him. The shadow wolves, however, found it an unpleasant experience, for where it touched them, they melted into nothing. Those that managed to escape now prowled the edges of the forest, keeping in the shadows, snarling and snapping their jaws.

Conor looked around and frowned. There were patches of blackness inside the circle of light.

"What in the name of Cernunnos?" he muttered.

"This is not good," Greymoon said.

"They can't enter the light," Conor said, turning to watch warily. Briefly, he glanced towards Rhoyd, who stood with the heel of his staff touching the ground, his forehead leaning against the wood, his eyes closed as though concentrating. "What's not good about that?" Conor added.

"They know we are here," Greymoon snarled. "We

cannot take this light with us, or we will never find the demon. It will only come in shadow."

Conor frowned at her. "I thought the whole idea was to put it back into shadow."

"We cannot with all this light."

"If he lets the light go, they will attack," Conor insisted.

"Can he push the light out?" Greymoon asked. "Is he strong enough to fill the woods and destroy them all?"

"Rhoyd?" Conor said.

Rhoyd took a deep breath and nodded. His limbs were trembling. It was clear that pulling power to do this was a strain.

Why? Conor wondered. *He's ne'er been so weak before...*

But it was as though the lad was having trouble holding himself up, much less pulling essence to feed his spell. And then it occurred to Conor. Rhoyd stood in a circle of dark.

Conor carefully walked over to where Rhoyd stood ringed in white light. The lad's face was pinched with strain.

"Rhoyd, what's wrong?" he asked.

"It's a void," Rhoyd whispered. "I have to use my own essence..."

"He will drain himself," Greymoon said. "He must have a source of essence, or he will drain himself."

"Can't ye just step out of the void, lad?" Conor asked.

Rhoyd shook his head. "If I move forward, I'll lose the spell and have to start again and..." His small face twisted in pain.

Conor stepped closer, grabbing Rhoyd's shoulders.

"Take what you need from me," he said.

Rhoyd blinked. "That's blood magic," he whispered. "If I am not careful, I could kill you."

"Better death at your hands than the maws of those demons," Conor said.

Rhoyd shook his head. "No, I can't. It's wrong."

"We've got to do something," Conor said.

He glanced at Greymoon, but she shrugged. Conor looked back at Rhoyd.

"What if I carry you out," Conor said.

"I don't know. I have to concentrate..."

Frowning, Conor glanced at the Fearfaolan once more. He stepped back, slipping his sword into its sheath. The light of it winked out, and he felt uneasy not to have it in hand. Cautiously, he knelt behind Rhoyd so as not to make him drop the spear, and gently put arms around the lad.

"Just keep concentrating," he said.

Carefully, he picked Rhoyd up and felt the lad flinch. The light around them flickered. Conor froze. He took a deep breath and started to walk forward, worried that he might slip.

How far? He knew there was an edge to this circle of shadow in which they stood, but holding the lad in front of him made it hard to see that edge. Hard to see the ground at his feet too. He moved twice his own height. As he moved, he could feel Rhoyd trembling and shaking, panting like a hound on a hot summer day. Another few steps. Then Conor's foot touched a root, and he froze.

"Put me down," Rhoyd whispered.

Slowly, Conor lowered the lad. The moment Rhoyd's feet touched the ground, Conor felt a burst of power.

Rhoyd shouted *"Solus Mhor!"* again.

The power hit Conor like a punch to the sternum. He staggered back, nearly falling over. As he watched, the white light spread out brighter than before. The shadow wolves that had been creeping closer suddenly turned to flee as the white light filled the woods, illuminating every corner, even those filled with shadows.

Screams filled the night as the world turned white. Conor's eyes barely adjusted to the brilliance, and then just as fast as it had spread, it winked out. Rhoyd took deep breaths, glancing up at Conor. He grinned at the lad.

"Ye did it," Conor said.

"We did it," Rhoyd said, throwing arms around Conor.

Greymoon moved close. "They are gone," she said. "Now, we must move on quickly before the Cu' Deamhan has time to find us."

"I thought we wanted to find the beast," Conor said, letting go of Rhoyd.

"Not here," Greymoon said. "Now come. Brown Chaser will have to carry Rhoyd again."

Conor made a face at the Fearfaolan. But there was little else they could do now. He helped Rhoyd to crawl onto Brown Chaser's back once more, and Conor took the rear this time as he drew his sword again and hid it under his plaidie.

Greymoon took the lead, and he let her. He wanted to be ready just in case anything came at them from behind.

It was need that called to Eithne for most of the evening, but now as she placed comfrey on a fresh wound and bandaged it in place, she realized that the need had dissipated to naught. A relief, to be sure.

She was starting to like the Fearfaolan. Odd as they appeared, they were not very different from humans. Indeed, some of the mothers let her hold their newborn pups, and some of the children danced around, tussled, and played. One of them brought her food on a wooden trencher, and to her surprise, it was cooked meat. She thanked them and ate it as she wandered back to the place where she and Conor and Rhoyd were supposed to be sleeping.

Empty beds greeted her. She paused.

They've gone without me, she thought.

Why? Why would they do that? Leave her here without so much as a good-bye.

She sighed and put the platter down and stormed off to the entrance of the cave. Some of the Fearfaolan looked uneasy to see her so agitated.

"My husband. My son? Did they pass this way?" she

asked.

Those guarding the entrance shrugged and pretended not to understand her.

"Fine," she said and marched on towards the opening that led out into the night.

"You would be better off to stay here," a familiar voice said.

Eithne turned to see the Fearfaolan called Goldmane walking up the corridor in her wake.

"And why is that?" Eithne demanded.

Goldmane did not look as though she were the least bit concerned that Eithne was taller than she. The Fearfaolan woman squatted and pointed towards some of the marks that were etched into the tunnel walls.

"Can you read them?" Goldmane asked.

Eithne shook her head. Letters--yes, she had learned them, and she could read and write, but the ancient marks on the walls meant nothing to her.

"They tell the tale," Goldmane said as she rose and started towards the entrance of the cavern.

Eithne followed. "What tale?" she asked as they stepped out of the cavern. Goldmane crawled up onto a ledge of stone that gave them ample view of the mountain rising like a silhouette in the moonlight.

"The lore keepers made those marks so we would remember and be ready," Goldmane said. "Your son is the Light of the World. He will be the one to bring back the light when darkness falls on the land. But to do so, he must stay alive, and to do that, he must go there."

She gestured towards the dark height of the mountain.

"And you expect me to wait here and do nothing?" Eithne asked. "While my husband and son face danger?"

Goldmane rose swiftly and grabbed Eithne's arm with surprising strength. For a moment, Eithne feared the Fearfaolan was going to shove her off the ledge. The fall would break bones for certain.

"Know this, mother of the Once Born Twice Blooded," Goldmane said sharply. "You must live so that you may keep the Light of the World alive. Out there, you would not live."

"How can you be sure of that?"

"You are a healer," Goldmane said. "You are not one who can give death without feeling guilty. Out there, you would be a distraction to your man and your son. The man knows death. I could smell it on him. He has made death many times. The lad knows death as well, but it is the death of all things dark and dank--all things that would turn this whole world into a place of shadows and bring the Dubh Sealgair and their Dark Mother back to rule with pain, terror, and death. They are the ones who must go. You are the keeper of life, and you must stay, and so I have sworn. Until they return, you will stay here."

Eithne looked into those lupine eyes, uncertain for a moment. She opened her mouth to refute the creature's claim that she was incapable of giving death, when the side of the mountain turned white.

"Oh, my," Eithne said and stared at a rush of white light that seemed to spread far and then vanish.

"And so it begins," Goldmane said. "Now come back into the caves and wait with the patience of your kind."

Goldmane's grasp slipped away as the Fearfaolan gestured back towards the cave.

"And if I refuse?" Eithne asked.

Goldmane made a yipping noise, and suddenly the sedge around the cave burst to life. More than a dozen Fearfaolan warriors appeared as though they had stepped through gate spells. Eithne gasped and backed towards the cavern mouth.

"They have orders to tie you to a stone if they must," Goldmane said and started back into the cavern. "But I gave my word, and they will not harm you otherwise. Do not force them to obey my commands."

Eithne held her place. A couple of the Fearfaolan crouched as though ready to spring. One female moved closer, baring teeth.

With a sigh, Eithne crossed her arms and stalked back into the caves.

"Blessed Brother," she muttered. "Please watch over them and bring them back to me alive."

She followed Goldmane back into the caves, though in her heart, she wanted to go the other way.

Once they had left the woods, Greymoon led them up the steep slope, picking a seemingly impossible path among broken boulders and the rubble of walls. That there had been a war here was clear to Conor. He'd seen enough battles and their aftermaths. Some of the stones bore the shapes of men--or creatures resembling men. Some looked more like animals.

As he passed one, Conor reached out and touched it. Even through his gauntlet, the stone felt unnatural under his hand, like he brushed something barely alive. He paused long enough to look at the shape. It was a woman whose face stared back at him, her head thrown back in some form of battle cry. She had carried a sword and wore armor that fitted her form, though time and the elements had worn some bits away. Still, that she was both a woman and a warrior was clear. Conor arched one eyebrow.

He had ne'er heard of a woman going to war. Well, except for that caravan cook they met whose name was Noreen and claimed she was descended from the bloodlines of someone called "The Hammer Maid." But then she had said she disguised herself as a man so she could go into battle. On the other hand, his auld nurse used to spin tales of battles and now and again there were battle maidens as fierce as any man. And through the course of his life, he had met many a woman whose skills went beyond hearth and home. Why even Eithne had a warrior's heart under that calm healer facade. Conor had seen it often enough.

Conor broke off his study of the stone and glanced back in the direction from whence they had traveled. The moonlight washed over mounds and moors and stones and trees, and barely afforded him a view of the mountain where he knew his wife was probably cursing his name. Briefly, he smiled.

Keep yer knickers out of a knot, woman, he thought.

No doubt the Fearfaolan were hearing no end to her blethering about being left behind.

Conor looked back around towards the summit they climbed. Greymoon and Rhoyd were pulling too far ahead for his liking. A few more steps, and he would lose them. He quickened his pace, eager to catch up with them, when something lashed across his ankle and sent him sprawling in the dark. He bit a curse as he felt a stone strike his chest in the sternum. Conor's vision flashed red in pain. He stayed down for moments longer than might be wise, he told himself, waiting for the pain to subside. Several deep breaths passed before the sensation fell away, and he crawled to his feet again.

And hissed, "Horns," under his breath.

Neither Greymoon nor Rhoyd was in line of sight now.

"Horns," Conor muttered again, and swiftly charged up the uneven hillside. Born in the highlands of Seanbrae and trained by the High King's Militia in the Highland Ranges, he was no stranger to hills or stones. But there was the dark to contend with, even though the moon cast a baleful light that washed the world blue. Conor lacked the lad's night vision. He could not hear either of them ahead of him and he scrambled across rough ground and tried to dodge stones in an effort to find the pair. It was not like Rhoyd to move silently, for he still had a lad's clumsiness about him, but he was riding that damned wolf, and no doubt the beast and its Fearfaolan mistress were used to moving as quiet as the moonlight.

He stopped as his lungs started to ache. There was a mist forming on the mountain ahead, obscuring the way.

Tempting as it was to call out to them, he dared not.

Conor hurried on, hoping that he would not get lost--

hoping above all that he would find them before the lad met a terrible fate.

Rhoyd watched as the mist began to thicken around them. Mage senses tingled as he pushed them out to search their surroundings. His head spun a little from the effort as well, and it worried him. Had he truly drained himself trying to conjure light within the ranges of that void? He hoped not. He had a feeling that what lay ahead was far worse than shadow wolves.

Briefly, Rhoyd laid his head down on Brown Chaser's neck and listened to the beating of the wolf's heart, the panting of his breath and the near-mute thump of his paws on the ground. An eerie silence was falling on the world around them. Not even Conor's footsteps could be heard.

Rhoyd raised his head suddenly.

He could not hear Conor at all.

Turning so he could look back over his shoulder, he saw that the mist had formed a thin curtain over the trail below, depriving him of the view. Conor was not there at all.

"Greymoon!" Rhoyd hissed. "Brown Chaser, stop!"

The Fearfaolan stopped, her ears flattening against her head in agitation. For a moment, he thought she might be about to lunge at him. Even Brown Chaser hesitated and took a few halting steps back and wagged his tail. But then Greymoon straightened up and started back down the rise at a slower pace.

"What is it?" she asked.

"Conor is missing," Rhoyd said. "The mist has cut him off."

Greymoon glanced back down the trail and sniffed. "He has fallen behind, drat him." Her eyes narrowed and she sniffed again, wrinkling her nose as though something did not please her.

"It's not his fault. It's the mist," Rhoyd insisted. "It came up suddenly."

She cast a surly glance at Rhoyd, and then shook her head.

"I will go look for him," she said. "You stay right here and do not move. Brown Chaser will keep you safe."

Rhoyd frowned. He didn't like the idea of being left here alone, even if he did have the wolf to protect him. There was something unnatural about the mist.

She started down the path.

"Be careful," Rhoyd called as softly as he could.

The Fearfaolan glanced back and offered a smile. "I will, little pup. Guard him well, Brown Chaser."

Brown Chaser turned so he was facing downhill. The wolf whined a little but stayed where he was. Greymoon moved on, slipping into the thickness of the mist, and vanishing from Rhoyd's sight. The wolf whined again, tail lowered, shifting back and forth nervously, ears flicking towards the mist.

"She'll be all right," Rhoyd whispered, though whether for the wolf's benefit or his own was uncertain. He rubbed one hand through the thick mane of Brown Chaser's neck.

A low, throaty growl suddenly floated up out of the mist. Rhoyd tensed as the snapping of jaws and snarling of canines filled the night. Brown Chaser whined and lowered his head just as a gut-rending yelp filled the air.

"Greymoon!" Rhoyd called, not caring who heard.

Another yelp rang amid the snarls of a lupine battle that must have been taking place. Had she run into another shadow wolf? Rhoyd was torn between rushing into the mist or staying where he was. Brown Chaser made the decision for him. A third horrendous yelp of pain echoed under a growl. Brown Chaser yipped and bounced and dove forward. Unready for the shift of his mount, Rhoyd was tossed back over the tail of the wolf as Brown Chaser dashed madly into the mist, snarling and snapping.

And then silence filled the air. Rhoyd crawled to his

feet, snatching up his staff, uncertain what to do next, when he saw a form in the mist. Upright and short, it lurched into the clearing and paused, shaking like a dog and sending flecks of blood spraying the area.

"Greymoon," Rhoyd said.

The Fearfaolan was covered with blood. She wiped an arm across her dripping jaws and stood there heaving, staring at him.

"Did you find Conor?" Rhoyd asked. "Brown Chaser ran before I could do anything."

She raised her hand to indicate silence. Blood ran down her arms. Without a word, she walked up the rise.

The stink of death and blood met Rhoyd's nose. He took a step back, uncertain.

She merely passed him and gestured for him to follow.

"But Conor?" he said as she moved on. "And Brown Chaser..."

Once more, she stopped, glowering at him, and gestured for silence, then moved on, indicating that he should follow.

He glanced back down the hill. What had happened out there? Where were Conor and Brown Chaser? Perhaps she had sent the wolf to find the man, but would Conor follow Brown Chaser back? He wished she would say something to reassure him.

With a sigh, Rhoyd glanced back up the rise. She was standing there, watching him, patiently waiting.

Glancing once more at the mist below, Rhoyd followed.

He just hoped Conor and Brown Chaser were close behind them.

And whatever Greymoon fought out there in the mist was not going to waylay them.

Conor was battling his way up the hill, tripping over stones and sedge, when he heard a low growl in the mist, followed by a canine battle.

Horns, I am not there for him! He pushed himself harder, heedless of the ground.

Yelps of pain and howls and snarls exploded. Conor picked up the pace, waving hands and sword in front of him just to keep from running into any of the standing stones. The ground did everything in its power to stumble him, and there were times he was crawling, barking his knees, grateful that kilts alone were out of fashion.

Then at once, the noise ceased, and the sound of something loping up the hill away from him faded.

Horns. Was he too late?

Conor pressed on, his lung screaming in protest. He hated to admit he was not as young as he used to be. There was a time when this sprint would barely wind him. He told himself it was fear for the lad that was stealing his breath as much as the climb.

The odor of blood now came to him, and he stumbled over a small body before his mind could make sense of it. Conor fell as the creature gave a grunt and a gasp, and landed on his hip, rolling over to see what had brought him down.

Even with the mist, there was a milky film of light on the world, and it revealed the shape of someone whose entrails lay sprawled across the ground. At first, Conor did not recognize the features, for the creature's face had been bitten and savaged. But the armor it wore reminded him quickly enough.

"Greymoon?" he hissed.

She barely opened her eyes, her vixen jaws spread, revealing teeth bloodied in battle.

"Go," she said and weakly gestured. "There is naught you can do for me now. The Cu' Deamhan has stolen my form. With the scent of my blood essence, it can deceive him. It will take the Ard Magister and use him to free its master, and then kill him."

"What?" Conor looked up into the mist.

"Be swift before it leads him to his doom," she said softly. "Be swift..."

She closed her eyes. Conor put a hand on her shoulder

172

and gave her a gentle shake, but she did not stir. He put a hand on her chest, and it came away bloody.

There's naught ye can do fae her, Manahan, he scolded himself. *Go find the lad.*

He pulled away from her, scrambling to his feet--and froze.

Something was moving out of the mist towards him at a lope. Raising his sword, he waited for it to come.

But instead, it stopped just a few meters away, lowering its head, teeth showing but not bared. It was the wolf called Brown Chaser who stood facing Conor now.

"Horns, where's Rhoyd?" Conor muttered.

Brown Chaser moved slowly, circling Conor, moving towards the Fearfaolan's body. The wolf sniffed her, and she barely moved, her hand touching his muzzle.

"Go, help him," she hissed and closed her eyes again. "Take him to the boy."

Her body grew still. Brown Chaser threw back its head and howled in remorse. Conor tensed, not daring to move as its eyes wandered back to him. Loping back around the Fearfaolan, Brown Chaser moved towards him now. The wolf lowered its head and tentatively wagged its tail, reminding Conor of the old wolfhounds they had kept at Seanbrae when he was a lad. Cautiously, he extended his hand, presenting the back of it as his father had taught him to do when one of those monstrous beasts approached.

Brown Chaser moved closer, pushing his massive hand under Conor's hand as though accepting him. Conor took a deep breath and crouched, petting the wolf as he would a dog.

"Here, lad," he said. "I'm sorry for the loss of yer mistress, but now I must go find my lad."

Conor rose and started up the rise. The wolf, however, seemed to have other plans. It rushed around and blocked his path and snarled.

"What, friendly one moment and my enemy the next?" Conor said and raised his sword, ready to kill the wolf if

173

necessary.

Once more, Brown Chaser lowered its head as though submitting, moving closer to Conor. But then, to his surprise, as it ran its head under his free hand, it suddenly took hold of his wrist in those powerful jaws. Conor started to shout--and then realized the grasp was more like a hand trying to lead him.

"All right, Brown Chaser. You know the way, aye?"

The wolf tugged. Conor relented and let it draw him in a slightly different direction from the one he had started to take.

"So we go that way?" he asked and gestured with his sword.

Brown Chaser let go and shied from the blade. But then the wolf started off in the general direction it had tried to drag Conor.

"All right, lad. Lead me to Rhoyd. If you understand me, lead me to Rhoyd.

The wolf stopped and looked at Conor, and then started on.

Conor followed, hoping this was not a wild chase he was being led on.

Using the staff to support himself, Rhoyd stopped on the trail and took deep gulping breaths. The mist was thinning, and so was the air, it seemed. But a heavy malaise hovered all the same. Already, he had seen signs and marks that he distrusted. Runes warning of death and destruction. Glyphs of protection and repellence. And signs of a great battle that turned some stones to slag and left others shattered. The air tingled with magic, and none of it felt good. He had cast about him with mage senses, trying to locate Conor, but all Rhoyd felt was death and voids. A hint of the Fearfaolan's essence was there as well. It was scattered about him, even up in front of him. In the midst he sensed the vague bitterness of a demon.

Ahead of him, Greymoon paused and look back, and

briefly, Rhoyd swore her eyes took on a bloody hue. Sort of the way an animal's eyes did when hit with light.

Strange, there is no light here.

As if reading his thoughts, she turned away and gestured that he should continue. He stood watching as she nearly disappeared, then with a sigh, he followed.

It was then that he noticed that beneath his feet, the path was a set of old, worn stone stairs, and some of the rubble and slag had once been part of a wall.

We must be in the keep. Rhoyd paused and put one hand on a stone.

Cold swept his senses, and copper filled his nose and mouth.

Blood magic! He quickly pulled his hand away from the surface, looking up at the wall.

Shadows wafted and waned like a fog there.

He wished Conor were here. And Brown Chaser. There had been a sense of comfort riding the wolf that was now totally gone, and Rhoyd started to tremble.

I cannot go up there alone, he thought.

Greymoon suddenly came trotting down the stairs. She glared at Rhoyd, and once again, he was struck by the odd coloration of her eyes. She gestured for him to follow, looking impatient.

"I want to wait for Conor and Brown Chaser," Rhoyd whispered.

Greymoon's ears went back, and she growled in displeasure. Rhoyd brought the staff around more by instinct than intention, and as the dragon's head nearly clipped her nose, she jerked back and growled more openly.

Rhoyd backed up, staff at the ready.

"What is wrong with you?" he asked.

She turned away from him and ran up the stairs.

"Greymoon!" he hissed. "Wait!"

But she did not wait. She barreled on practically on all fours, and all he could do was follow. And this time, he felt the chill of desperation at being deserted.

He charged up the stairs, heedless of the noise he made, determined to catch up with her.

At the top of the stairs was the archway like the one in his dream. The familiarity struck him so swiftly that he nearly stumbled over the shaft of his own spear. Rhoyd stopped. He was standing on the edge of a wide flat area, and at its center stood a megalith arch whose center was dark. Greymoon was nowhere to be found, but his annoyance at her was forgotten. He cautiously crossed the expanse to approach the stones.

There were marks here, both ancient and familiar. Figures etched into the stone showed a man standing next to a wolf nearly as large as a horse. Rhoyd blinked. The man was thin with long hair. Around him were the runes of lightning and fire. The figure's gaze was cast across at the opposite side of the arch. Rhoyd moved that way and found a second set of drawings. A man carrying a spear with several beasts at his side, glowering back and behind him, a sun whose rays spread shards of light like spearheads. Peering closer, Rhoyd realized that the beasts had bodies like humans. Fearfaolan, he thought. One wore armor, a female like Greymoon, only taller. She stood at the forefront, glaring at the thin man on the other arch, and in her hand was a sword.

So, this was the story Greymoon had told him, of how War Mother and her son faced the Shadow Lord. Rhoyd studied the runes once more, trying to cipher the ones he could remember seeing in books from his uncle Fenelon's hidden library. Haltingly, he read them.

This is the gate that holds back the darkness.
This is the gate that waits for the key.
Blood of the light shall open the way
And set the darkness free...

Rhoyd stepped back with a gasp. This was what Brina had told him.

176

It was her blood that set the demon loose.

And now the blood of the light shall open the way...

My blood?

A snarl alerted him. Rhoyd turned ready to strike out with the spear.

Greymoon stood not far away, but now she was dropping to all fours, shaking like a wet hound, and her body was shifting and growing in size. What was it Fenelon once said? Demons are not limited by their natural size as mageborn are. When they shift into another form, they can be as large as a house or as small as a flea.

Rhoyd's heart thundered. He tore the dragon off the end of his staff, revealing the spearhead as the beast that once looked like Greymoon became the creature of his worst nightmare.

TWELVE

Eithne sat near the mouth of the cave, watching the Fearfaolan warriors patrolling the bluff that overlooked the rise of the moors, the distant woods, and the mountains. She hated this waiting, not knowing what was happening to husband and son.

Goldmane came and sat at Eithne's side; sword laid on the ground at her own feet. Eithne tried not to scowl at the Fearfaolan, but she was in no mood for company. Still Goldmane remained as though not the least bit worried that her presence was unwelcome. Besides, she was pricking her ears towards the night in a worried manner. And ever so faintly, Eithne sensed need in the Fearfaolan, but it was not the need of injury or disease, but the need of unease.

"You don't look happy," Eithne said with a sigh.

"There is a scent on the wind that I do not like," Goldmane replied, and her ears twitched again. She suddenly bounded to her feet, snatching up her sword and glaring at the night. The Fearfaolan guarding the cave entrance stiffened, hackles going up on some shoulders and backs. "I smell death," Goldmane whispered.

It was then that the lonely howl of a wolf echoed from across the moors, and the Fearfaolan warriors took up the call. Their voices boomed into the cavern, and from the depths, Eithne heard the cacophony of many voices raised in the same mournful song. She put her hands over her ears to protect them from the deafening sound when Goldmane added her howl to the rest.

"What is it?" Eithne shouted. "What is wrong?"

179

Goldmane looked up at Eithne, and there was a glint of remorse welling in her lupine eyes.

"Brown Chaser says Greymoon has fallen."

"Fallen?" Eithne repeated.

"She has met her fate in battle and now dies on the field of her honor."

Eithne felt her heart go into her throat. "What of Conor and Rhoyd?" she whispered.

"They go on," Goldmane said.

"Without her to guide them?" Eithne glared at the Fearfaolan.

"There is naught they can do for her," Goldmane said. She stepped out of the cavern towards the band of warriors. Eithne followed swiftly.

"Two of you," Goldmane said. "Find Greymoon if you are able and bring her back here so she might be among her descendants. And be careful of what hides in the mist."

Eithne stopped at the edge of the bluff, gazing towards the mountain. *Conor! Rhoyd! Oh, Blessed Brother, give me a sign.*

But none was immediately in the offing. She watched as two of the Fearfaolan warriors with swords tied across their backs bolted off across the moor, crouching on all fours to aid their speed.

And wished she could follow.

Conor felt clumsy compared to the wolf that dashed ahead of him. Now and again, Brown Chaser would stop and look back as though perturbed. Conor would stumble, often going to his knees, and he knew they would be black and blue by the time this was over. But he would get up and go on, knowing there was a reason somewhere up in the mist of the mountain.

For somewhere up there was Rhoyd, all by himself facing only the gods knew what.

And ye couldn't be bothered to bring him with ye when

yer mistress was attacked, could ye? Conor thought. He remembered the Fearfaolan had told the wolf to protect the lad at all costs. *Now what would yer mistress think of ye?*

Conor frowned and wondered why he was arguing with a wolf when another stone caught his toe and tripped him. He barely stayed upright this time, flailing for balance on the uneven rise. Horns, but he had not run the Highlands since he joined the militia, and now he felt as clumsy as a flat dweller from Gwyrn.

Brown Chaser stopped again and looked back, ears flat.

"I'm doing the best I can," he growled through gritted teeth. "Give me credit, will ye?"

Brown Chaser waited until Conor caught up. He stopped, looking around.

"So where is the lad?" Conor asked.

Brown Chaser pushed his head under Conor's free hand and nudged against him as well.

"What are ye wanting from me now?" Conor asked.

The wolf pushed, knocking Conor off balance, and he instinctively grabbed a handful of the thick mane of hair over the wolf's shoulders to keep from falling. Brown Chaser suddenly took off with Conor in tow.

"What in the name of Cernunnos!" Conor let go and nearly fell. The wolf circled and came back under his hand and pushed against him again, forcing Conor to grab fur once more.

And then it dawned on him.

He's trying to help me! By the Horns, he's trying to help me climb this mountain.

This time as the wolf sprinted forward, Conor clung tight. The wolf ate the ground in powerful strides, but it was keeping to a path that Conor would follow without tripping, as though knowing what stones to avoid in the dark. As a result, Conor put down his head and ran, heedless of footing, finding trust in the wolf's greater skill at seeing in the shadows and the mist.

But then the ground changed, and Conor realized he was climbing stairs carved into rock. They broke out of the mist and through a gate of ruins, faced with more stairs.

From above, Conor heard a clatter and a shout and a howl. The noise echoed all around him as though there was a full pack of wolves in the mist.

He let go of Brown Chaser and ran full tilt up the stairs towards the sounds.

The demon before Rhoyd began to howl, and its cry filled the night. From near and far, lupine voices answered. The mist curled and undulated and spat forth more of the shadow wolves. They formed a semi-circle behind the beast, their eyes glowing with unnatural fire.

Rhoyd tightened his grasp on the spear, holding it before him as Conor had shown him. He kept trying to remember over and over in his own mind the lessons of the last few days. Remember, lad, it's not a sword, but it can cut just as deep. Rhoyd took a deep breath and crouched, letting mage senses reach out for essence. White fire. He needed white fire to keep them at bay.

But in this place, essence was spare, and his own was dwindling. He sensed that the mist was like a void, covering places and hiding the power therein. *Just a little essence--please--just a little essence somewhere!* He searched for it, not daring to take his eyes off the beast and its shadow minions.

"There is no power here, Ard Magister," a voice whispered in the wind. "At least none that will serve you."

Rhoyd blinked. He looked into the beast's balefire eyes, uncertain. Demon, yes. The bitter tang of that essence brought bile to his tongue. But speech? How could it speak? He brushed it with mage senses again and nothing more than demon essence and a mad hunger assailed him.

Who had spoken to him?

The hairs on the back of his neck prickled like needles sticking in him. A faint wind, fetid with death and decay, began to draw across his back. Rhoyd risked a cautious glance over one shoulder towards the archway.

Blackness filled the opening, tinged around the edges by red and green flashes of dim light. Magic sang to Rhoyd's blood, a song of immortality and darkness.

It's a gate! he thought as he shifted his grasp and turned a little more. A spell gate.

Suddenly the words on the archway made more sense.

"Yes," a voice whispered from within the writhing ichor that formed in the center. "Your blood--your death--shall set me free."

"No," Rhoyd hissed.

He stepped away from the gate, only to hear the ominous thump of paws behind his back. With a shout he turned and slashed at the dark form lunging for him. The head of the spear turned white as it opened a wound in the shadow wolf as it rushed him first. The beast yelped and dissipated into a mist. But even as it fell, another hurried forward to take its place. Behind it, Rhoyd could see that the demon was conjuring more shadow wolves. Rhoyd was forced to step aside and lash out again. This shadow wolf twisted out of reach, dropping to the ground as another came darting across the broken cobbles and flagstones and rubble.

Rhoyd stepped back and let the creature impale itself on his spear. It howled and disappeared like the first, but as it did, a third shadow wolf appeared. He took another step back only to feel cold breath on his neck. With a shout, he threw himself off to the side, barely avoiding the paws that would have shoved him into the gate spell.

Laughter echoed from the depths of the gate. Rhoyd barely glimpsed a shadowy form--a man tall and handsome with sinister eyes. A mere shadow of his living presence, but Rhoyd could feel the dark power surging through the image.

"Close," the being whispered. "But it is your life and

blood that I need to escape this prison. Kill him!"

Rhoyd scrambled to get his feet under him. His hand touched a bit of earth, and through that small opening, he felt the essence of the stones beneath.

There is essence in everything, Fenelon once told him. Even the smallest bit of it can help you.

Rhoyd yanked it to him, feeling the strength of stone. He pulled the power into his soul and snapped to his feet, and with a cry of triumph, he closed his eyes, raised the spear and shouted, *"Solus mhor!"*

Stone gave him the strength to push forth a ball of white light so that he stood in the center of a sun. It spread swiftly, eating away the dark mist. He heard howls and screams of pain as his power ate away the shadow wolves and turned them to dust.

Their howls died with them, and Rhoyd opened his eyes.

An orb of darkness stood before him, rolling towards him like a great boulder. He sensed demon essence at its core, and it was bearing down on him rapidly, pushing aside his light.

He shouted and brought up the point of the spear just as the great orb of darkness lunged at him. There was a screech of pain and a howl of anger from within the darkness of the arch as black ichor sprayed, stinging him with its acidic presence.

The orb faded and revealed the Cu' Deamhan impaled on the end of his spear. But it was not dead. Indeed, it writhed and lashed at him with claws and biting jaws, forcing him to back down the spear and try to keep it at bay.

"Your blow was not true," the Shadow Lord chuckled.

Rhoyd tried to brace the spear against a stone just to keep the beast from pushing him back into the gate. He dug in his heels and hung on for all he was worth, but his limbs began to tremble and shake with exhaustion.

Oh, horns, what do I do?

184

But it was then that he heard a voice shout, "Get away from him!"

The demon turned with a snarl as a sword glowing with white fire swung at its head.

The mist had parted and revealed the flat area encircled in the rubble of ancient walls. Conor took only a moment to scan the scene. Before him, he spied the arch of stones and the shadowy figure that waited beyond, but immediately before them was a beast with a spearhead protruding from its back, and just beyond was Rhoyd, holding onto that haft for dear life.

That was all Conor needed to see. He raised his glowing sword and charged the creature, shouting.

The beast turned, throwing Rhoyd off balance as the lad struggled to keep hold of the spear. The face that met Conor was like that of a wolf, but unlike one of the Fearfaolan, this creature was all hairy and gnarled, as though someone had taken a wolf and tugged it into a terrible unnatural shape then left it in a grave to molder. Conor thought no more of it and struck with his sword, intending to cut off the hideous head.

His blade bounced off the hide, though the fiery spell that made it glow left a burn mark.

Snarling, the monster practically ripped Rhoyd's spear out of its chest and turned to attack.

Horns, it was a demon, and Conor's steel, though ensorcelled with the magic fire, was unable to cut that hide. The monstrous thing lunged at Conor, forcing him to scramble backwards. He took another swing at it, futile as it was, and this time the beast snagged his blade in one claw and howled as the white fire burned its skin. But it would not let go, and with a mighty lurch, it tore the hilt from his grasp. Conor backed away again and went for the shorter blade glowing on his hip. Jaws snapped within inches of his face, and only training and instinct saved him from losing his head. Conor drew out the short sword and lunged at the monster's chest, but the beast

185

merely slapped the blade aside, knocking Conor off balance. One of its claws grabbed him by the throat.

A snarl burst from his left and Brown Chaser charged into the fray. The wolf's jaws clamped down on the arm that held Conor. The demon howled, though Conor doubted it was truly hurt. Surely wolf jaws were no better against a demon's hide than his own steel.

But Brown Chaser had weight as well as a strong grasp, and the wolf's attack threw the demon off balance. It released Conor and turned its attention to the wolf, snarling as it flung the brave creature aside. There was a frightful yelp as Brown Chaser hit the stone wall and landed in a heap.

Conor took advantage of the demon's distraction to eye the distance to his long sword again. It lay against one of the stone figures. Conor practically flew towards his glowing steel when his progress was cut short by a claw snagging his chainmail and tunic from the back. His feet left the ground as the demon yanked him back around towards it. Conor kicked and flailed, shouting at the monster, hoping to find some vulnerable place.

And then he heard a youthful shout, and a gleaming spearhead burst through the demon's chest. Snarling, it dropped Conor and turned towards its attacker. Conor landed on his feet, staggering as the shout turned into a startled wail. He glanced aside in time to see Rhoyd clinging to the haft of the spear, riding it towards him as the demon spun about to try and grab the boy. His smaller body slammed into Conor who grabbed the shaft of the spear in stronger hands.

"Hang on, lad!" Conor shouted.

The demon was still turning, driving them towards the very stone Conor had been trying to reach to fetch his sword. He clung to the haft and raised his feet, catching the stone under his boots. The motion jarred him to the bone, but it jarred the demon as well. The shift of the spear opened more of the wound and sent gouts of black ichor across the ground. Rhoyd yelped as a spot of it splattered his hand and sizzled like water on rock. The lad nearly let go of the haft of the spear, but even in pain, he clung to the wood as though it meant his very life to do so.

The demon screamed and writhed on the end of the spear, twisting this way and that, trying to grab the haft. And just when Conor thought they might triumph because it could not twist its arms around, those limbs became as limp as dough, and then snaked around behind the beast to seize the haft close to Rhoyd. Conor let go with one arm, yanking the lad close to him and the beast jerked the haft of the spear and pulled it free once more. Conor and Rhoyd were sent tumbling, still clinging to the spear. They landed on the ground with mutual "huffing" sounds.

The beast turned with a snarl, ichor still running rivulets down its chest.

"Yes, my pet. Take both their lives and use their blood and deaths to set me free." Even Conor heard the voice that issued from the gate.

"Not on my watch," Conor snarled.

He scrambled to his feet, pulling Rhoyd with him as the demon surged at them. The spear was still in Rhoyd's hands, but it was Conor who guided it now. He felt as he did when he killed Keltoran boars, watching them charge at him, an unstoppable force.

The spearhead went into the open jaws and drove straight up into the creature's brain. The demon's flight was cut short, but its momentum still drove them back into one of the standing stones. The haft of the spear caught on a stone, and the spear went on through the demon's head, leaving it dangling there like a moppet.

For a moment, neither Conor nor Rhoyd moved as the creature convulsed, and then grew still.

There was a shout of rage from the open archway. Its darkness swirled and shrank and closed.

"We are not done with you, Ard Magister. We will find

a way to destroy you before the next Darkening, this I promise."

"Not if I have anything to say about it," Conor said. He heaved himself away from the stone, knocking the demon's corpse off to one side and began to work the spear free. Then he stood back and waited as Rhoyd called white fire in the mage tongue and set the demon's body afire. Then the lad summoned a wind to lift the ashes and slam them against a stone of obsidian marked with runes. As Conor watched, the black stone drank in the remains until there was nothing left except for smoke, and the scent of decay and sulfur. The wind carried it all away with the mist that now fled the mountain heights, leaving Conor able to take a deep breath and look at the glitter of the stars.

The darkness was full of the yips and growls of the Fearfaolan. Eithne had returned to the mouth of the cave to sit and wait. Goldmane insisted Eithne should return to the inner sanctum and go to sleep, but there was no sleep as far as Eithne was concerned. She could not have slept had she drunk one of her own draughts. Not knowing what had become of husband and son had every nerve in her body standing on end.

The noises from the forest and the moors began to change. And grew louder as someone moved closer to the caves. Eithne climbed onto one of the outcroppings that would allow her to see the trail.

Fearfaolan broke out of the forest, and in their midst, a tall man carrying a small form.

Rhoyd? Oh, no, Blessed Brother. Don't let it be Rhoyd!

Heedless of the night that could have easily disguised the treacheries of the path, Eithne bolted down from her perch and hurried along the trail. Other Fearfaolan were coming out of the caves behind her, and a cacophony of howls began to fill the night. Mournful sounds, they ground into her ears, making her want to fly faster.

She came down a dip in the trail and started up a small rise and stopped. Conor was more visible to her now, and the small form in his arms dangled like a useless rag. His face was as stoic as it had been the day their son was killed.

Oh, Blessed Brother, no, she thought as she watched him stop on the trail. She put a hand to her own chest, tears springing into her eyes, when a small figure moved out from behind him, leaning on a staff, guided by a wolf that was limping.

Eithne blinked.

"Rhoyd?" she said softly.

The lad looked up at her. His face was covered with dirt, and he had a makeshift bandage on one hand. His need spoke to her in volumes, and the urge to throw her arms around him and call Diancecht's healing power was strong. But she saw the look on Conor's face, and the bundle that he carried.

"She died well," he said. "Like a true warrior."

Eithne's eyes drifted down to the ravaged form of the older Fearfaolan.

"I'm sorry," she said.

Conor nodded, his face remaining unreadable.

Fearfaolan gathered and took Greymoon from him, and bore her on into the cave. They streamed past Eithne and her little family in silence now. Only Goldmane stopped at Eithne's side.

"She will be treated with honor and sent to join the Ancestors by becoming one with us," Goldmane said. "And you and yours are welcome to join the funeral feast."

"I think we'd just as soon get back on the road and move on," Conor suddenly said.

"As you wish," Goldmane said and took off after the dwindling crowd.

"Let's get our gear and horses and leave," Conor said.

"But Rhoyd needs..."

"A good night's sleep," Conor said, and he slipped one arm around the lad's shoulder and drew him close. "We will get the horses and the packs and go back down the trail to the woods to camp."

"Will it be safe?" Eithne asked.

"Aye, the demon beast is dead, and the gate is closed," Conor said.

"But shouldn't we stay until Greymoon is buried?"

"I would just as soon not be around when they start their funeral feast," Conor said.

"Why not?"

"They don't bury their dead, woman. They eat their dead," Conor said.

Eithne glanced up towards the caverns. "They eat their dead?"

"It's a custom, they tell me," Conor said. "Not one I care to partake in, just so you know."

"Let's get the horses," Eithne said.

Conor nodded and started up the rise, still holding Rhoyd to support the lad while Eithne and the wolf followed.

EPILOGUE

Rhoyd was reading his book when he got the impression he was being watched. He lowered the volume and turned in the saddle to look.

High up on the rocks he made out the figure of Brown Chaser basking in the glow of the afternoon sun. After they had gathered their gear last night, the brown wolf had followed them back from the Fearfaolan stronghold and into the woods, and no amount of shooing from Conor or Rhoyd would make the wolf leave.

"She told him to protect me," Rhoyd had said when Conor tried yet again to shout and drive Brown Chaser away.

"Aye, well, the last thing we need is a wolf following us about," Conor replied. "See if ye can speak to the beast and tell him just that."

Rhoyd sighed. He had no idea how to speak to the wolf so that he would be understood. But at least Brown Chaser had wandered off into the forest and left them alone.

For the night...

Come morning, as they rose for the day, the wolf was sitting just a short way off watching them. Conor snarled an oath and tossed a stick at Brown Chaser. The wolf merely dodged it and returned to trailing after them as they mounted up and took to the highland road.

"We could say he's a dog," Rhoyd suggested as Conor sat glaring at the beast when they stopped to water the horses. "After all, he has no one else now that his mate and Greymoon are both dead. She did tell him to look

191

after me. Maybe he's just lonely?"

Conor did not look amused, and Rhoyd stifled the desire to say more. But then Conor sighed.

"He's a wolf, lad, and there isn't a man from here to Wenthorn that won't know it."

Rhoyd tried not to look disappointed. They mounted up and rode on, and still Brown Chaser followed, never too close, but never out of sight.

The sun was going lower, and Conor picked a camp. Rhoyd started a fire. Conor trapped a few rabbits and skinned them as Eithne prepared tea and set out pallets. Silence surrounded them as they each did their part to prepare for the night.

Soon the rabbits were roasting on the spit, and Conor was amusing Rhoyd with a story about the time he and his brother Finn tried to catch a rabbit in their auntie's garden when Brown Chaser suddenly appeared, dragging a small deer. Conor put a hand to his sword as the wolf brought the deer right over to Conor and laid it at his feet.

"Oh, my," Eithne said.

Conor frowned and glanced at Rhoyd expectantly. "Is that a peace offering?"

Rhoyd shrugged. "I guess," he said.

Conor sighed. "He's going to keep doing this until we accept him, aye?"

"I think the silly creature must believe you are the alpha in this pack," Eithne said, and Rhoyd saw that her mouth was thinned to keep from laughing.

"Well, he's right about that," Conor said firmly.

He poked at the deer and sighed.

"All right, I accept his gift," Conor said, "though now I've got to clean and gut it, and the meat is likely tainted, though the hide might be useful if it doesn't rot on us."

"Then he can stay?" Rhoyd asked.

"Aye, as long as he doesn't cause trouble," Conor said and offered his hand to the wolf.

Brown Chaser came over, head low, tail wagging, and

pushed his hand under Conor's hand.

"But there is going to be a problem when we get to Wenthorn," Conor said and rubbed the wolf's head.

"What?" Rhoyd asked.

"Meg," Conor said. "I don't know that she's going to be happy with a wolf spending the winter in her barn."

"He could stay in the room with me." Rhoyd suggested.

"Let's not push it, lad" Conor said.

He pulled one of the rabbits off the spit and offered it to Brown Chaser. The wolf snatched it from his hand and settled down by Conor's side to eat.

Rhoyd couldn't help but smile.

END

About the Author

Laura J. Underwood has been writing stories as far back as she can remember. She started writing when she was a child (because her mother told her talking out loud to herself made her sound crazy). Laura also realized that by writing down her daydreams, she could read and relive them over and over. As a result, she excelled at writing assignments in school, and would write and share those stories with her closest friends for entertainment, usually based on her favorite television shows.

She was also an avid reader, devouring books like candy. Her parents and other relations kept many books, and as a child, she was allowed to read whatever she could get her hands on. She had access to everything from Bulfinch's Mythology, Shakespearean plays, various encyclopedias, Edgar Rice Burroughs, and H. Allen Smith to Edgar Allan Poe, as well as her mother's gothic novel collection. And she learned quite early in life that if she stayed quiet as a child, her great grand parents would not force her to leave the room so she could hear all the old stories of their East Tennessee family roots. Story telling just came naturally.

Her career as a published writer started when she sold her first article to *Fate Magazine* as a teenager, followed by several nonfiction sales. In fact, her first paying job was as a stable bum (a groom in a private boarding stable, but she always called herself a "super duper pooper scooper") which led to her writing and selling articles on horses, training, and stable work. When she left the stables, she took a job as a library page, eventually

195

becoming a librarian, working her way up the internal ladder (where she honed her research skills as a writer). She became a regular book reviewer for the *Knoxville News-Sentinel*, even writing a few author interviews for the paper. And in the interim, she has been an artist, a camper, a hiker, a fencer, and a fencing coach.

She continued to write fiction as well, and in the mid-eighties, she sold her first short story, *Sword Singer,* to Marion Zimmer Bradley for SWORD & SORCERESS V. Laura started selling fiction regularly to small press magazines and to various anthologies.

In 2000 at ChiCon, while fencing as a SFWA Musketeer, she met writer/publisher Selina Rosen. They traded humorous verbal barbs over rubber chickens and rubber rats, fenced together, and became fast friends. It was Selina Rosen who invited Laura to submit short fiction to the BUBBAS OF THE APOCALYPSE anthologies, as well as her first novel ARD MAGISTER to Yard Dog Press. Since that time, Laura has published numerous novels, including DRAGON'S TONGUE, WANDERING LARK, HOUNDS OF ARDAGH and several collections of short fiction about a certain Harper Mage. She and Selina are the coauthors of the BAD LANDS series of gonzo mystery novels.

Currently, she is a retired librarian who still writes. This novel SHADOW OF THE FAOLAN is the third in her series of adventures about Rhoyd Smytheson, the Ard Magister, and his adopted family. Yes, she plans for there to be more while she works on other projects and still sells short fiction to online magazines from time to time.

She can be found expounding on the writing life and reviewing books on her Facebook page (facebook.com/keltora) as well as showing pictures of meals and her sewing and art projects, and the various ball jointed dolls she collects.

About the Cover Artist

Stephen Parks, aka: CheetahRyu, received his BFA in graphic design before receiving a Master's degree in Illustration from the Academy of Art University. He helped in a mural project for the Fort Smith, AR civic center in 2002 before starting his freelancing business. Originally called SP GraphiX, Stephen soon changed the name of his business to his on-line handle, CheetahRyu.

Today, Stephen's clientele are mostly from the Fort Smith, AR area. He prefers to work closely with his clients to ensure they receive quality artwork, but he also sells numbered prints of his work that can be shipped if needed and many graphic and digital art packages can be commissioned from anywhere. Steve has published three adult coloring books and written a YA novel; *Brownies in the Attic.*

Like his Facebook page: https://www.facebook.com/cheetahryu, where you can also view some of his work. Feel free to contact him through his FB page.

Yard Dog Press Titles at This Printing

Rosen

Texistani: Indo-Pak Food from a Texas Kitchen, Beverly A. Hale

That's All Folks, J. F. Gonzalez

Through Wyoming Eyes, Ken Rand

Tranquility, Tracy Morris

Turn Left to Tomorrow, Robin Wayne Bailey

The Twins (#4 in the Sword Masters Series),, Selina Rosen

The Undead At My Head, Ethan Nahté

Villains in Training, Julia S. Mandala and Linda L. Donahue

Wandering Lark, Laura J. Underwood

Weirdough, Inc., Selina Rosen and Sherri Dean

Wings of Morning, Katharine Eliska Kimbriel

Zombies in Oz and Other Undead Musings, Robin Wayne Bailey

Fantasy Writers Asylum (A YDP Imprint):

Blood Songs, Julia Mandala

Chaos Heir: Beholden A. D. Guzman

Death's Paladin Christopher Donahue

Gateway to Corimar, Julia Mandala & Linda L. Donahue

Spirit Poles, Julia Mandala & Linda L. Donahue

Tale of the Black Heart, Linda L. Donahue

Traitor's Gate, Linda L. Donahue & Julia Mandala

Double Dog (A YDP Imprint):

#1:
Of Stars & Shadows, Mark W. Tiedemann
This Instance of Me, Jeffrey Turner

#3:
Home Is the Hunter, James K. Burk
Farstep Station, Lazette Gifford

#4:
Sabre Dance, Melanie Fletcher
The Lunari Mask, Laura J. Underwood